J. T. EDSON'S
FLOATING OUTFIT

The toughest bunch of Rebels that ever lost a war, they fought for the South, and then for Texas, as the legendary Floating Outfit of "Ole Devil" Hardin's O.D. Connected ranch.

MARK COUNTER was the best-dressed man in the West: always dressed fit-to-kill. THE YSABEL KID was Comanche fast and Texas tough. And the most famous of them all was DUSTY FOG, the ex-cavalryman known as the Rio Hondo Gun Wizard.

J. T. Edson has captured all the excitement and adventure of the raw frontier in this magnificent Western series. Turn the page for a complete list of Berkley Floating Outfit titles.

J.T.Edson

GUNSMOKE THUNDER

BERKLEY BOOKS, NEW YORK

Originally printed in Great Britain by
Brown Watson Limited.

This Berkley book contains the complete
text of the original edition.
It has been completely reset in a typeface
designed for easy reading, and was printed
from new film.

GUNSMOKE THUNDER

A Berkley Book/published by arrangement with
Transworld Publishers Ltd.

PRINTING HISTORY
Brown Watson edition published 1963
Corgi edition published 1969
Berkley edition/January 1985

ISBN: 0-425-07459-5

A BERKLEY BOOK® TM 757,375
Berkley Books are published by The Berkley Publishing Group,
200 Madison Avenue, New York, New York 10016.
The name "BERKLEY" and the stylized "B" with design are
trademarks belonging to
Berkley Publishing Corporation.
PRINTED IN THE UNITED STATES OF AMERICA

GUNSMOKE THUNDER

CHAPTER ONE

Nogana

It wasn't the biggest ranch in the West. Red Blaze was grudgingly willing to concede that point, but by cracky it was going to be the best.

There was always a surge of pride hit Red as he rode towards the small cluster of buildings which formed the living quarters and the center of the S-B Ranch. They, the buildings and this land belonged to him and his partner Johnny Raybold, late scout of the Wedge trail crew.

The ranch buildings were not much, nothing to eyes which had seen the haciendas of old Mexico or the great house of the O.D. Connected spread in the Rio Hondo country of Texas. Just two small frame cabins facing each other about twenty yards apart. Beyond them lay the small bunkhouse, a big barn and stable, a blacksmith's forge which backed to a small stream which ran by the property. The three corrals were stoutly made, laying behind the bunkhouse; there were only a few horses in for the ranch did not have need for a large remuda at the moment. From between the two cabins ran a wagon trail which headed straight to the county seat, Apache City, a small town six miles away.

Red, riding in his low horned, double girthed Texas saddle with the easy grace of a cowhand, allowed the big claybank stallion to make a better pace towards the house. The horse, a cross between a sorrel and a dun, with a yellowish coat, was big, fine looking and powerful, a speed horse, a go-to-town horse but of little use for cattle work. It was Red's special favorite and he always used it for anything other than working cattle.

He was a typical Texas cowhand, this Red Blaze, tall, wide shouldered and without an ounce of fat on his powerful young frame. The brown Stetson, expensive, fitted to Texas style and set at the right "jack-deuce" angle over his off eye, hid a thatch of fiery red hair and shielded a freckled, pugnaciously handsome face from the sun. Red's eyes were blue, merry, laughing eyes in the tanned face. His mouth was strong but looked as if it would rarely be without a cheery grin. Around his throat, tight rolled and knotted, was a bandana in which every conceivable color warred in a glorious riot. He was prouder of that bandana than of any other thing he owned, except for the blonde and beautiful little girl he called his wife. The bandana had been a gift from his uncle, Ole Devil Hardin, to celebrate his first lone hand chore for the floating outfit* and Red treasured it for that. His shirt was dark blue, his levis brown and showing signs of being pressed, not a usual thing in the days before his

*Told in *The Hard Riders*.

wedding. Around his waist was a brown leather gunbelt and butt forward in the holsters were a brace of walnut handled .45 Colt Cavalry Peacemakers. From under his leg showed the butt of an old Spencer carbine, a battle-field capture from the days of the Civil War when he rode as a lieutenant in the Texas Light Cavalry.

Red saw his wife emerge from their cabin and raised his hand in a wave, the young woman replied to it and Red gave a guilty start. He reached hurriedly behind him to make sure the large package fastened to the cantle of his saddle was not in view of the house.

Sue Blaze, small, petite, very pretty and blonde, stepped from the porch of the house and raised a hand to shield her eyes from the sun as she looked towards her approaching husband. For once she was wearing a gingham dress instead of jeans and a shirt-waist. No matter what she wore she was a pretty picture, her face heart-shaped, the eyes blue and twinkling with a love of life as great as her husband's, nose small, the lips full and looking as if they were made for laughter. Her hair was short, curly and generally looked, as did Red's, as if the feel of a comb and brush were rare.

By now Red had reached the corral and he swung down, taking care to keep the package from his wife's view as she approached, stamping her feet down in a determined manner which he knew well. He hid the pack-age behind the stoutest post of the corral fence and as-sumed a look of injured innocence as he turned to face his wife.

"Howdy, honey," he greeted.

"Huh, Texans!" Sue grunted disgustedly. "I know I shouldn't have married one. 'I won't be long, honey,' he says. Not much he wasn't. Been gone near all day he has. Leaves all the work—"

"It was all Johnny's fault," Red answered, laying the blame on his absent partner's head. "He—"

"Went out to the foothills by the reservation first thing this morning," interrupted Sue, then plumbed his other excuses before he could make them. "Billy Jack's down there riding the south line. Young Frank's clearing that waterpole on the lower forty and Tex's on the east line."

With that Sue put her hands on her hips and looked defiantly at Red, daring him to talk his way out of it. Red was licked and he knew it, for he could not now lay the blame on the other male members of the S-B Ranch. There was only one thing left to do.

With a quick lunge forward Red scooped Sue into his arms and planted a kiss full on her lips. He felt the hard firm muscles under the rich full curves of his wife's body straining against his arms. She let out a startled yell as she saw she was being carried towards the stream.

"Red Blaze!" she shrieked, knocking his hat back to hang on its storm strap, then digging her strong fingers into his hair. "You dare drop me in the creek! I'll tear every hair you've got out!"

The door of the Raybold house opened and Betty, Mrs. Johnny Raybold, stepped out, watching them with a tolerant smile. She was Red's cousin.

Sue and Betty were much alike in some ways, exact opposites in others. They were the same size and had the same rich, full shapely figures. They were both extremely pretty young women but Betty's was a different kind of beauty. Sue looked warm, friendly, just a little innocent and naive. Betty was more maturely beautiful, her face showing breeding, self-control and intelligence. Her black eyes were friendly, yet more serious than Sue's. She wore a tartan shirt-waist, a pair of washed out blue denim pants and had Kiowa moccasins on her feet.

The two young wives got on very well despite or, perhaps because of, their different upbringings. Sue had been raised on a ranch in Arizona, a small place and her education came from lessons given by her mother and father. Betty had been an orphan from her second year, she'd been born and raised on the mighty O.D. Connected Ranch of her grandfather, Ole Devil Hardin. Her education had been by private tutor and then in a fancy Eastern school and she was a couple of years older than Sue. Betty brought one restraining influence to the partnership, her husband, though none of his old friends of the Wedge would have believed it, supplied the other. For all that it was a true partnership, working and, more difficult, never allowing Sue to feel that she was not a full member of it. In fact in many ways Sue was pleased that the ranch was run in such a manner. Red was skilled with cattle but he was not a good businessman.

"Are you pair at it again?" Betty asked as she approached. "Say, Cousin Red. How about heading for the foothills and seeing if you can scare Johnny up for me. He went up there this morning just after you pulled out and hasn't come back."

"You mean he missed a meal!" asked Red incredulously, setting Sue on her feet and planting another kiss on her face.

Betty nodded in agreement. Her husband was a trencherman of note and she'd been very surprised when he did not show up for a meal. It was unlike Johnny to miss food without good cause although she was not seriously worried. The S-B was a new spread and there was much work to be done on it.

Apache County, New Mexico, had orginally been owned by two feuding families, with a tough old-timer called Comanche Blake running a cap-and-ball outfit up in the foothills by the Lipan Apache reservation. The Dobies and the Groutens feuded to such cause that in the end not a living man of either family remained. The Governor of New Mexico Territory, to prevent further feuding and to regain lost tax money, ruled that the land of both families be taken over, split into half a dozen smaller spreads and put up for sale. Smaller was a relative term, for each of the spreads was the size of a small Eastern county.

That was where Red and Johnny came into it. They bought this spread, registered the S-B Ranch brand and set out to make it pay them. On their west line they had Comanche Blake's daughter, the old man had died shortly before Red's arrival in Apache County; on the east line a Bostonian gentleman called Colonel Akins. This same Akins brought a party of friends from the East with him, intending that they should occupy all the local ranches but they arrived too late. There had been some hard feelings over this, for two members of the Akins party failed to get a ranch.

While Johnny, the two girls and their tophand, Billy Jack, came along from Rio Hondo with two wagons of household goods and a small herd of whiteface cattle, Red made a fast ride. On his arrival he hired two tough, handy young Texas cowhands to help with the work— and work they did. They'd worked twelve hours a day, riding the ranges and, with the aid of Comanche Blake's daughter, her two grizzled old cowhands, and a couple of old-timers from the Apache County area, built a second frame cabin.

Early after his arrival Red found things were as he suspected. The Dobies and Groutens had been too busy feuding and killing each other to take any care of their herds so the range was covered with unbranded cattle, and was the property of the first man to lay his brand on it. Red and his two young hands had worked the range as well as they could manage and the S-B brand was slapped on many a bull, cow or calf.

On Johnny's arrival the work went ahead fast and the S-B now ran a good herd in which the whitefaces were mingling to improve the strain of beef. Red and Johnny had made tentative suggestions to the other ranchers that they all combine to sweep the country from the reservation foothills to the county lines and gather in all the stock. The round-up would be handled thoroughly, the cost of it borne by all the ranches and the unbranded stock shared out equally. The suggestion was not greeted with any enthusiasm, for the Eastern people did not know the cattle industry and were inclined to look down their noses at the S–B owners and crew.

So it was that only the Stirrup Iron and the S-B that prospered, for the others were owned by people who did not know the cattle business and were worked by milk-cow hands who had come from the east with the owners. Rapidly they were becoming a problem to the owners.

"Reckon I'd best take out and scare him up then," Red drawled and grinned at Betty. "I'd bet he was over to Comanche Blake's, sparking her."

"Not Johnny," answered Betty, for she knew there was no reason for her to mistrust her husband, even with a girl as pretty as Comanche Blake's daughter. "He's too noble, too loyal, too scared I'd find out and beat his head in with a broom. Get going, Cousin Red. By the way, was there any mail for us?"

"Nothing. Anyways, there's not likely to be since we heard from Uncle Devil that he was sending us a bunch of bloodhorses to run on the range."

With that Red turned back and swung afork his claybank, pulled his hat back on to his head and reached for the reins.

"Don't think you've got away with it, Red Blaze!" yelled his wife. "I'll still want an explanation when you get back."

The two young women watched Red ride away then turned to each other.

"Did he get it?" Betty asked.

"He sure did. Got it hid out down by the corral. Let's go take a look."

The girls strolled to the corral and fetched out the large neatly wrapped parcel. They felt it, prodded it with their fingers and finally Betty asked:

"Do you reckon we could wrap the parcel up as neat as this again? I'm terrible at making up a parcel and from what I recollect you're not much better."

"You just about called it right," Sue agreed, then snorted angrily. "Don't it beat all git-out how awkward men can be? Now we'll have to wait until they decide to show us."

Betty smiled and agreed. By devious methods, thinking their wives did not know why they wanted them, Johnny and Red had managed to get Sue and Betty's dress sizes. They'd sent to an Eastern mail-order house for two party dresses the girls had been admiring in the dream-book the company sent out. There was to be a big ball at Apache City at the end of the month and the S-B ladies must look their best for it. This morning Red had headed for town and collected the dresses thinking neither girl knew anything about it. In that he was real wrong, for the girls both knew, and had hoped to get a sneak look at the dresses.

"Are you all right?" Betty inquired glancing sideways at Sue as they replaced the package. "You look just a mite peeked and I saw you heading for the back-house real early this morning."

Sue's cheeks reddened slightly. "I'm all right. Least I think I am. I might only be a couple of days late in starting."

With that Sue turned and headed for the house. Betty watched the other girl go and a gentle smile played on her lips. She was thoughtful as she headed for her house to start preparing a meal for the hands when they came in.

Red found no trouble in picking up his friend's trail. Johnny was riding his big iron grey stallion, his favorite mount. The S-B did not run a big remuda, not more than twenty horses altogether, so Johnny was using his personal mount and saving the better trained cow-horses for when there was more work. Red was curious as he followed the tracks. There must be something important in Johnny's non-return. His partner would sooner pat the head of a diamondback rattler than miss a meal. If something urgent had come up Johnny would welcome a chance to have help.

The range through which Red rode was good for open-grazing. The grass was deep, lush and fattened cattle well. There was plenty of water and enough bushes and trees to give shelter to the cattle in any kind of weather.

Red's eyes went to the rim of the hills which surrounded the Lipan Apache reservation. He wondered if the Apaches would stay at peace and on the reservation. Burton Hillvers, the reservation agent, thought and said they would not. This proved little in Red's mind other than the Indian Bureau's lamentable choice of agents. Hillvers was a big, florid dude and although in charge of the Reservation Agency never went near the reservation if he could avoid it and spoke not a word of

Apache. Comanche Blake's girl was firm in her belief that Hunting Wolf, supreme chief of the Lipans, would keep the peace. Red was inclined to believe the girl, for she knew Indians, her mother had been a full blooded Comanche.

The claybank stopped and Red jerked erect in the saddle, his right hand twisting palm out to close on the walnut grip of the right side Colt. With the seven and a half inch barreled Cavalry Peacemaker in his palm Red rode through the bushes and looked down at the dead body of a pony which lay at the top of an arroyo. It was a small, dainty paint, better than the usual run of the Indian bangtail. From the lack of a saddle Red guessed it was an Apache pony and he looked around for its owner.

A woman screamed from inside the arroyo. It was the scream of a woman in terror and Red rode nearer, dropped from the saddle, allowed the reins to hang free in front of his claybank and went to the arroyo edge. He ignored the dead pony for a moment and looked down the very steep slope to the scared face of an Apache girl as she lay on the sand at the bottom. The arroyo was a dried out water-course, some twenty feet wide and perhaps fifteen feet deep. The action of the water which once flowed along it carved down into the soft ground to leave this scar, open and clear bottomed. Red saw the marks the girl had made as she went down. She must have been riding the horse when it fell and had gone over the rim.

She was Apache, Red saw that in one glance. A girl slightly taller than Sue, with black shoulder long hair done in braids and held back by a headband. Her face was less heavy nosed and thick lipped than was usual in an Apache woman, pointing to a mixture of Spanish blood in her veins. Her figure was good and the white doeskin dress with the porcupine quill decorations was not that of a poor woman. There was a broad silver bracelet around her right wrist with an ivory hilted knife at her left side. Her moccasins were knee-high doe or calfskin, and Red knew that she was more than just some stray squaw. He saw that in one glance, but his attention was more on that writhing shape which moved towards the girl. It was a big rattlesnake and Red guessed the girl's legs must have been hurt going down the slope or she would have moved away.

There was no time to think about anything other than ending the life of that snake. There was no time to even turn and draw the Spencer carbine. Red knew he must depend on his skill with the Colt.

Bringing up the Colt, Red gripped the butt in both hands as he lined it down and sighted it carefully. There would not be time to spray much lead, the first shot must count. The sights lined, Red squeezed the trigger and let the hammer fall. The big Colt kicked back against his hands, powder smoke hid the target for a moment, then cleared. To his relief the snake was thrashing in two pieces, the .45 bullet had struck home.

"Lay easy there, gal," he called. "I'll get you out."

Going back to his horse, Red took the sixty foot length of three strand, hard plaited Manila rope from his saddlehorn. He made one end secure to a tree trunk and tossed the other down the slope. Even with the aid of the rope it was hard to go down the steep side of the arroyo without falling and Red could see the girl had been lucky to light down without even more serious injuries.

The Apache girl watched Red with something akin to fear in her eyes. Her left hand went to the hilt of the knife. No Apache ever trusted a white cowhand.

"Do you understand English, gal?" Red asked, not moving nearer until he was sure he would not get that knife into his body.

"I do."

"You wouldn't be Nogana, Hunting Wolf's gal, now would you?" asked Red, for he was even more sure that here was no ordinary Apache squaw.

"I am."

"Comanche Blake told me about you. She allowed you'd been to an Eastern mission school. Say, let's take a look at that leg."

Nogana's hand came from the knife hilt and Red breathed a sigh of relief. The girl had heard Comanche Blake's daughter talk about the men who ran this ranch, she could trust them. That was why she'd taken the short-cut across their range on a visit to Comanche Blake's house. Some instinct told her this red-haired ride-plenty did not have anything to do with her being in the arroyo.

"It is my right ankle, I think it is sprained," she said, then glanced at the still writhing shape of the snake. "But could we get out of here first, please?"

"Why sure."

Red took the loop of his rope and passed it over the girl's shoulders, down and under her armpits. Drawing the loop up tight Red told the girl to grip the rope firmly over it and try to prevent it getting tighter. He carried her to the base of the arroyo side and set her down. Gripping the rope where it hung down Red climbed up to the top, turned and called to Nogana to hold tight. Then he took a firm hold of the rope and began to draw it up hand over hand. It was a second before the slack was taken up and the weight of the girl came on the end of the rope. She was not light and it was far from easy to draw her up the slope. Sweat poured down Red's face but he did not stop hauling. The rope must be biting into the girl, hurting her, but she gave no sign of it.

Feeling as if his lungs would burst and that he could not do anything more, Red saw the girl's head appear over the top of the rim. Her arms were on the top and she helped by dragging herself up until she was on the top. Red sank down by her side and shook his head. He waited until he caught his breath then asked:

"What happened to your horse?"

"He was shot."

"Shot!" Red barked. "Who did it?"

"That I do not know. I found a wounded man and was trying to locate your ranch to get help. I think somebody shot at me although they hit my horse. I felt it fall and threw myself clear. I went on the side away from where the shot came and slipped over the arroyo edge. I hurt my ankle and lay still."

"How long ago was that and what wounded man?" demanded Red.

"About half an hour as I know your time," she replied. "The wounded man is less than a mile from here. He is a ride-plenty like you, with the same color hair."

Red came to his feet, all thought of rest gone. A ride-plenty, a cowhand with red hair. There was only one such in the whole of Apache County. Johnny Raybold was a Texas ride-plenty and his hair was a fiery thatch which matched Red's own.

"If I get you on my horse will you show me?" he asked. "I'll fix your foot first."

"On your horse I will not need a foot," she answered. "Lift me there and I will show you to your friend."

Red carried the Apache girl to his horse, swung her up on to the saddle, then mounted behind her. The big horse seemed to sense the urgency of the situation for it strode out at a good pace. Red handled the horse, following the girl's directions until he saw the still shape under the shelter of a bush. There was no doubting it was Johnny Raybold.

Dropping from the saddle of the big claybank Red ran forward and went to his knees by Johnny's side. The handsome face was pallid under the tan, the eyes closed. His shirt had been torn open and his shoulder was wrapped in a bandage. Red saw this and felt grateful that Sue and Betty always insisted the men carried clean white cloth in their saddlepouches ready for just such an emergency. The Apache girl must have opened the pouches to look for something with which to bandage the wound. She had done a good job of it from the look of things.

Red could see there was nothing he could do except get Johnny back to the S-B house as quickly as possible. His eyes went to the ivory handled Army Colt in Johnny's holster. It was an old model of gun, percussion fired, one of the fine Civilian pattern the Colt company made between 1860 and 1873 when they started to produce the Peacemaker. Johnny carried it and would not change to a cartridge fired weapon for anything. It was a considerable surprise to see the gun was still in the holster. Red's eyes went from the revolver to Johnny's horse, then to the Indian arrow which lay by Johnny's still form.

Rising, Red went back to his horse and helped the girl down. He sat her on the ground and drew the moccasin from the injured foot. The ankle was badly swollen and Red felt suddenly sorry. He opened his own saddlepouch and took out strips of cloth. Like most men who rode the range, Red knew something about treating injuries and his bandaging of the ankle was skillful.

"Who shot your hoss?" he asked.

"I do not know. It was a Sharps rifle, or one of the

heavy ones, not a Winchester. I know the difference."

Red nodded. The Sharps rifle was something few cow-hands carried. They preferred the lighter, handier, though shorter ranged Winchester repeating rifle to carry on their saddle.

"What sort of arrow's this?" he went on, picking up the shaft and turning it over in his hands.

"It is not Lipan," Nogana answered a trifle defiantly and angrily.

"I never thought it was. Happen I didn't know there wasn't any in this neck of the woods, I'd call it a Ute hunting arrow."

"As you say, there are no Utes in this part of the country," agreed Nogana. "I have never seen one and no Lipan would use a Ute arrow, it would be bad med-icine to do so."

"That's all right, gal," drawled Red. "I didn't allow any of your people had done it. Fact being, I was real sure of it."

"How can you be so sure?" she asked.

"Waal, I reckon you'd have made sure I didn't find the arrow if it was Lipan. And from what I've heard tell about them no Apache'd leave a hoss as good as the grey behind. Even if he did he wouldn't be likely to leave Johnny's belt gun, even if it is a beat-up ole relic like this. And even if by some real strange chance he did leave the Colt he surely wouldn't leave that—"

Red pointed to the grey stallion and the Winchester rifle which was still in the saddleboot. No Apache would leave one of those wonderful, light sixteen shooting rifles behind. He would take it and sing praises to his gods all night for his good fortune.

"It appears you know something of Apaches," the girl remarked.

"Know them the same way I know most Injuns," Red replied. "Fighting against them. Don't recollect ever having to fight Lipans though."

"The Lipans have never fought against the white-eyes and I pray they never will do so," Nogana replied. "There are many voices among the young braves raised to join the Apaches of the West and fight the soldier-coats. They will make loud talk because my horse was killed and I nearly so."

"Yeah and there'll be hotheaded fools around Apache City who'll start yelling about Johnny taking an arrow. Don't worry none, gal. I'll see the truth gets told."

The Apache girl and the young Texan stood silent for a moment. Nogana was an intelligent young woman and had attended mission school. She knew little to make her trust white men but something told her that here was a friend.

"Look, gal," Red went on. "Take my hoss and head for the house. Tell my missus what's happened and ask her to get a wagon out here."

The girl opened her mouth to reply, then they heard a noise. Red came around with his hand twisting to the butts of his guns. Even as he did he saw he was too late. Five Apache braves stood in the bushes behind him and one of them already had his bow raised and an arrow ready to release.

CHAPTER TWO

Red Blaze Makes Friends

Red Blaze brought his right hand Colt out in a fast done cavalry twist draw but he knew he would be too late. He might get the brave but the arrow would cut in through his chest and kill him even as he fired.

Then the girl was standing before Red, arms spread out although her face showed the pain her ankle must be giving. She stood between Red and the Apache, his hand quivered on the bowstring but he held the arrow, for to release it would have sent it into the girl.

"No, Manuel!" Nogana snapped in Apache. "This is a friend. Lower your bow." The brave made no move to do so and her voice hardened. "I said lower your bow."

The warrior still made no attempt to obey the order. There was a slit-eyed killer look on his face that Red knew well. It was the look of a man with blood-lust on him, wanting to make a kill. Only the girl between them prevented the Apache from releasing the arrow.

Four of the Apaches were of the usual squat, thick bodied bow-legged and powerful type so common among their people. The fifth was taller, with a spread to his shoulders and a slimming down at the waist which hinted at great strength. He was naked to the waist and muscled in a way Red could only remember seeing one other man. His black hair was shoulder long, taken back with a red headband. His torso was brown and carried gun and knife scars. Apart from a loincloth and knee-high moccasins he was naked, and around his waist was a leather gunbelt with a walnut handled Army Colt in the holster. In his right hand was a Winchester rifle, one of the brass framed Model of 1866, the "yellow boy" which was still in production at that time. There was an air of command about him which told Red that here was a minor chief, a fighting leader of one of the Lipan warrior lodges.

This was proved, for the big Apache growled an order and instantly the bow was lowered, the arrow returned to its quiver. Then the big man spoke to the girl and his voice was strangely gentle after the hard growl.

"Who is this man, Nogana?" he asked, pointing towards Red. "Who is the injured one and why do you ride with them?"

"He found me after I had an accident," she replied. "He helped me. I had already found his friend and cared for an arrow wound."

Red listened without understanding. He did not speak Apache and the conversation was all in that tongue. The Colt went back to leather, but Red did not relax.

Before there could be any more talk they all heard the sound of fast running hooves. A horse tore through the bushes, ridden by a squat, powerful Apache. From the red headband and the deference shown by the other Apaches, Red guessed that here was Hunting Wolf, old-man chief of the Lipan Apaches.

"Shinqua!" boomed the newcomer in Apache. "Why are you off the reservation?"

"We searched for Nogana," replied the big brave.

The girl began to explain and although he understood none of it Red could guess she was telling her father what had happened.

At the end of the speech Hunting Wolf turned to Red, glanced at the way he stood, hands ready to whip out his guns.

"You have no need for weapons, Texas ride-plenty," Hunting Wolf said in fair English. "You save the life of Nogana, my daughter. Never need you fear the Lipan Apache, you or any of your people, from this day."

"Hear this now, Hawks of the Lipan," went on Shinqua, speaking in Spanish so Red could follow him. "This white-eye ride-plenty saved Nogana. The man who harms him or his people hurts Shinqua and will pay with his life. This I swear by the sacred oath of our lodge."

With that the big Apache changed his Winchester to his left hand, holding out his right in the white man's way. Red was no weakling, but he was willing to admit Shinqua was stronger than him. Stronger than any other Red had ever met, save one.

"It was nothing," he said, hand still tingling from the powerful grip. "I just happened along and saw the girl in trouble, so I helped out."

"There are many white-eyes who would not have helped," Hunting Wolf put in. "Can we do anything for you?"

"Why sure," Red agreed. "I'd admire to get old Johnny there back to home."

"That is easily done."

With those words the chief gave a series of short and guttural Apache orders which sent his men into the bushes.

"By what mark do you know your cattle?" asked the chief.

Red glanced at his horse, it carried the O.D. Connected brand and Johnny's was still carrying the one burned on when it became part of the Wedge remuda. He found a clear piece of soil and with his toe drew the S, the bar and the B. The two Apaches studied it for a moment then grunted.

"Never again will our people take cattle which bear that mark."

"How come your boys take cattle anyway?" asked Red. "I thought the agent supplied you with food."

"My people are often hungry. There is little game left on the reservation and the buffalo no longer come. We cannot live on the food of our fathers and must rely on what we were promised when we signed the treaty with the soldier-coats."

"You're not getting enough food then?"

"We are not," replied Hunting Wolf with quiet dignity. "The Lipan Apache are not Navajo to eat roots. We need meat, for that is the food for men. Your people made peace with mine early. We rode as scouts and fought against the Kiowa, Comanche, Waco, Kaddo and for it we were given this reservation and the promise of food. Now the agent does not keep his word and my young men are hungry. They say we should leave the reservation and join Geronimo in the West."

"That'd be plumb foolish," drawled Red.

"It would be foolish. If we leave the reservation, or take up the war-hatchet we will lose the reservation. I have seen the armies of the white-eyes. I have seen great cannon which can smash a village from beyond rifle range. I have seen the gun of many tongues which could cut down ten hands of warriors while they were loading a rifle. All this I have seen while riding scout for the army. There is no hope in war against the white-eyes. We must stay at peace—or die."

"Yeah," Red agreed.

While they were talking Red saw the other braves returning with branches of various lengths and thicknesses. These were handed to Nogana who started working fast to prepare a travois on which Johnny could be taken to the ranch.

"You haven't been getting the right amount of food then?" Red asked the chief.

"Less than half of what we are promised by the White Father in Washington's treaty."

"I'll go in and see Hillvers come morning," Red promised grimly. "If he's keeping back your food I'll see it's stopped."

"That could be dangerous," warned Hunting Wolf. "The agent has hard men working for him."

Red grinned, his hands brushing the butts of his guns as he thought of the three tough cowhands who rode for him.

"I've got me a fair answer to hard men, me'n ole Billy Jack both. Anyways I'll go along to the fort and see that young Yankee captain."

"I have seen him. He is very young and does not know the ways of the west or of the Indian Bureau. He has listened to the honeyed words of the Agent."

"I'll still talk to him," Red promised. "He's not the kind who'd stand for any crooked play."

The girl had by now finished the travois and she gave rapid orders to the waiting braves.

Johnny's still form was lifted gently and carried to the travois. The girl took a blanket from one of the braves and used it to secure the wounded and unconscious cowhand, then nodded to Red.

"Get your friend's horse," she ordered. "I don't think it would take kindly to my people handling it."

That was true enough. Johnny's big grey did not take to strangers and had been used on Indian scouts often enough for it to dislike and distrust the red man's scent. So Red led the grey to where the girl stood and the men lifted the shafts for Nogana to secure to the saddle. Red expected trouble, for the grey had never been used to anything like this and would not take it quietly. However, Nogana spoke gently and soothed the big horse and to Red's surprise it stood still.

With the travois arms secured the girl bounded astride the double-girth Texas rig and took up the grey's reins. Red expected all kinds of trouble, but the grey knew a born rider and the futility of fighting one. Looking towards her father Nogana nodded and he snapped an order which sent the five braves into the bushes to collect their horses.

"Did your gal throw a stick at Shinqua?" Red asked with a grin as he and the chief went to their horses.

Hunting Wolf turned his eyes to Red's face and a rare smile came to his face. The white-eye ride-plenty knew something of Apaches if he knew the custom of a girl wishing to be courted tossing a stick at the man of her choice.

"You know of that custom?"

"Some *hombre* called the Ysabel Kid told me about it. He knows more about Indians than anybody I ever met, up to and including Tom Horn and Al Sieber."

Once more the smile flickered on Hunting Wolf's face

for he knew both the men mentioned, they were the two leaders of the Apache Scouts.

"If he knows more of Indians than my brother Sieber and Tom Horn then he is truly an Indian."

Red chuckled, he'd often thought that of the Ysabel Kid himself. "His grandpappy's Chief Long Walker of the Comanches. A man'd say he knows some about Indians."

The sun was setting as the party started across the range and Red allowed the Apaches to lead him. It proved to be a wise decision. Red thought he had a fair idea of the country but the Apache had ranged over all of it, hunting and traveling, in the days before they were herded on to the reservation. So Hunting Wolf led the way to the Blaze house by the shortest and, for Johnny, the easiest route.

For all that it was dark by the time the lights of the ranch buildings showed ahead. It was not pitch black and Red could see his three hands sitting outside the bunkhouse. He could tell Billy Jack's long and doleful length even now and make out the tall gangling, good looking youngster called Tex who was plucking at the strings of a guitar and singing of the fate of poor Lil Joe the Wrangler who would never wrangle more. Young Frank, stocky, curly haired and with a lit cigarette hanging from his lips, sat to the side of the others plaiting a length of rope, a favorite hobby of his.

The song came to a sudden stop as the three men looked up and saw the riders approaching.

Frank's cigarette fell from his mouth as he came to his feet, the rope flying from him as he slapped his right hand to his Colt-less side. Tex was also on his feet, holding his guitar in one hand as the other went wildly to where usually his holster lay. Even Billy Jack, a hardy battle-tried veteran, started to make a draw.

Red saw the two youngsters whirl on their heels and let out a roar of:

"Quit that fooling and get over here, will you!"

At the sound of their boss's voice the two young cowhands slid to a halt. Billy Jack had already seen the travois and sprinted forward at a pace far different from his usual lethargic movements.

The doors of the two cabins were thrown open to show Betty and Sue. They both held a lantern in one hand. Betty had a Winchester carbine in her other hand while Sue lent her trust and faith to a twelve gauge shot-gun and a load of buckshot. Betty saw the travois and its burden behind her husband's grey stallion before Sue did. The dark haired girl neither screamed nor fainted. She came from the porch and ran towards the party, arriving a second ahead of Sue who showed as little sign of hysteria.

"What happened?" Betty asked, looking from Johnny's still form to where Red was swinging down from his horse.

"Johnny took an arrow but Nogana there fixed it. He'll likely live to eat us out of house and home."

Betty snorted, knowing the true feeling behind the apparently heartless sentiment of her cousin. "Which same's less likely than you and these three loafers sleeping us out of it." She turned her eyes to the cowhands. "Grab hold of that stretcher and get him to the house instead of standing there looking like screech-owls on a tree stump."

Billy Jack and Tex jumped forward to obey. They unfastened the travois and by the simple process of gripping the extensions, turned it into a stretcher on which they could carry Johnny into the house. Betty went with them and it was left for Red to introduce the Apaches to his wife.

Sue Blaze had been born in Arizona and lived there all her life. She'd seen Apache warfare and this was the first time she'd ever seen Apache close up without having to take cover and start loading weapons.

"It might be wise if you sent for the white doctor from Apache City," Hunting Wolf remarked. "My daughter is something of a medicine woman but she had nothing with which to work her medicine out there."

"See to it, Frank," Red snapped.

Soon after the Apaches left, they mounted their horses and the braves joined them. Hunting Wolf made a sign and they turned their horses to ride away. Nogana was seated behind Shinqua, she turned and waved her hand, but that was the only sign they gave.

Red stood with his arm across Sue's shoulders and watched the party ride away. Sue waved back in reply to Nogana, then looked at her husband.

"They never said good-bye," she remarked.

"The Kid allows they never do," he answered. "It's a funny thing. I never thought about any Injun as a human before today."

"Me neither," Sue answered. "Who do you think killed Nogana's horse?"

"I don't know, gal. Or who shot Johnny. It wasn't an Apache, that's for real sure. I wish Dusty was around."

"And me," agreed Sue.

The girl looked up at her husband, trying to read any reproach for her words. There was none. Red Blaze knew his limitations as well as his strength. He was a good fighting man, a better than fair shot although not fast with a gun. It took Red all of a second to draw and shoot, to be fast a man needed to halve that time. Red was not fast with a gun, but given a straight fight he could handle it. He was hot tempered, liable to jump feet first into trouble without looking where he was due to land. In a matter where planning and strategy was needed Red knew he was out of his depth. He could use the help of his most illustrious cousin, the Rio Hondo gun wizard Dusty Fog.

"Reckon I'm not much of a husband, honey, wanting help to fight my battles."

Sue laughed, turning her face up to him. "You're talking loco. Sure, Dusty would help and I wish he was here for that. But I wouldn't change my husband for a hundred Dusty Fogs."

Red kissed Sue then replied, "There couldn't be a hundred Dusty Fogs. They threw the mold away when they made him."

The doctor arrived shortly after midnight, riding a horse with the ease of a man who'd spent forty years of his life in the saddle, traveling to visit patients. He left Tex to care for his horse and headed for the house where Betty was waiting for him. Sue and Red sat on the porch of their home waiting until the door opened and the doctor came out with Betty. The three cowhands drew nearer to hear what was said, for they were loyal to their bosses.

"Don't know that you needed to send for me, although I'm glad you did," the doctor was saying. "Whoever bandaged that wound knew what he was doing, or was it your work, Mrs. Raybold?"

"I'd like to claim that honor, doctor," Betty replied. "But it was Nogana, Chief Hunting Wolf's daughter, who did it."

The doctor had long since grown past the stage where anything could surprise him. He knew that the Apaches had been using bows and arrows for many centuries and knew much about the care and treatment of arrow wounds.

"Anyway, he'll be all right. Let him sleep as long as he can and keep him in that bed for a fortnight, then no strenuous exercise for another week at least. I reckon you're strong willed enough to do it."

"She sure is," said Tex fervently, but he said it under his breath, for Mrs. Betty Raybold had a tongue which would blister the hide of a buffalo bull and was not particular about using it when she felt such was needed.

"There's coffee and some food down at the house," Sue remarked. "I reckon we could all use some."

The meal offered a good chance of swapping gossip and all were pleased to get the chance.

"Akin's losing stock," the doctor remarked. "Blames the Apaches."

"I'd lay he doesn't know how many head's on his land," Red answered. "If him and the others would throw in with us on a big gather there'd be some real surprised ranchers in Apache County."

"They'd need some cowhands instead of those dude boys they hire first," Sue put in. "I was out on our line and saw one riding alongside a steer and trying to lean over to get his rope on it. I never did figure what he aimed to do with it if he caught it. Anyways, he chased it right out of sight and still hadn't got the rope on it."

"They're not so bad, just need showing how to go on," Red drawled.

"I know how I'm going to go on," growled the doctor. "I'm going on to the bunkhouse and catching some sleep."

"We'll ride into town with you in the morning, Doctor," Red remarked. "Sue looks like she could do with a change and I want to see Hillvers."

The party broke up, Betty heading for her house and her husband, the cowhands going to the bunkhouse.

Red headed for the corral at a rush. He had just re-membered the parcel and wanted to get it to a safe hiding place. However, there was no sign of it by the post where he left it. Red made a thorough search, thinking that perhaps a coyote might have dragged it off. Then he went to the bunkhouse.

Seated on his bunk, resplendent in his red long-john underwear, Billy Jack gave Red a grin and jerked a thumb to the parcel which lay on a shelf.

"Come to collect this?" he asked.

"Sure, did you fetch it in?"

"Not me," lied Billy Jack, for he'd been given the parcel by Sue on his return from working on the range. Sue and Betty had given him orders that he must not let either of their husbands know they'd seen it.

Red took the parcel down and examined it. He'd seen the way Sue and Betty made up parcels and this was too neat for either of their efforts. He was puzzled as to how the parcel came to be in the bunkhouse. Tex and Frank were already asleep in their bunks and he did not wake them. One thing he was sure of was that Betty and Sue did not know the contents of the parcel.

"Where've you been, Red honey?" Sue whispered as her husband climbed into the bed beside her.

"Looking over the stock," answered Red. He'd given Billy Jack orders to keep the parcel at the bunkhouse and not to mention it to either Betty or Sue. "Tell you, honey. One of these days I might have a surprise for you."

Sue snuggled nearer to Red, sliding her arms around him.

"Good," she replied gently. "And I might have one for you."

CHAPTER THREE

Red Blaze Makes Plain Talk

Looking at Apache City a stranger, used to the larger cities of the East might wonder at, or be amused by, so grandiloquent a name. There was area to Apache City's limits which far exceeded that needed by the forty or so houses of the citizens which lay behind the glittering facade of Geronimo Street as the main, in fact only, street was called. Even Geronimo Street had pretentions to far greater length than was really necessary. The entire business section of the town, with the exception of one small house with heavy curtains at the windows and female company inside, lay along Geronimo Street. There was the Lipan Apache Agency, an imposing building standing in its own grounds, with a stable and large storehouse behind it. There was the sheriff's office, jail and county offices, all imposed in a wooden building which might possibly be strong enough to hold a crippled, weak midget prisoner. There was a large saloon, the back room of which served as a bank, for the saloon keeper was also town banker although he did little enough business and his big safe, shipped from the East when he thought the town would boom, rarely carried a great amount of money. The houses, like the business premises, were a mixture of wood or of adobe, and even the meanest of them stood in its own grounds.

To one end of the town was Fort Apache. Again this was a somewhat grandiloquent name. Fort Apache had been built in the days before the Civil War and once held a full regiment of cavalry permanently as its garrison. Now, with the reduction of forces and the urgent need for men further West only a small battalion under the command of a captain remained. Fort Apache had no wall around it, other than a four foot high stack of adobe brick which surrounded the buildings. The barrack blocks, the officers' quarters, the guardhouse with its stockade, the Suds Row where lived such of the enlisted men who chose to bring their wives and families with them, the storehouses and the horse lines were well maintained. This was to the credit of the Commanding Officer. Captain Randolph van Sillen might be younger than was usual for a three bar these days, he might be fresh from a desk job in Washington, but he knew how to make his men work and did not intend the fort to fall into decay.

It was into this thriving county seat, coming along the well marked trail which led on to Geronimo Street, passing the large building which served as meeting house, dancehall or anything else that civic needs called for, that Red Blaze, his wife and the doctor arrived shortly after noon. The doctor was riding his horse while Red and Sue sat on the box of the small two horse wagon. The girl handled the reins and Red sat with his Spencer carbine across his knees. That was the way in the West, the woman handled the ribbons and left her man's hands free to use his weapons in case of an attack.

Red was puzzled, he hardly spared a glance at the meeting house where the two barbecue pits had been cleared out ready for the dance at the end of the month, no more than eight days away. What puzzled Red was his wife's attitude. Her sudden rushing to the backhouse every morning for the past three days. The way she had tried to put off riding to town with him. A trip, even in to Apache City, was usually something Sue looked forward to.

For her part Sue was worried and not a little scared by the thought of what was happening to her. She wanted everything to go off all right although she was not sure how Red would take the news when he finally heard. She decided to put off telling him until after the dance as she didn't want him fussing over her and stopping her attending.

The doctor turned his horse to head for his home which lay at the back of the town. He raised his hand in a salute and grinned at Sue:

"Don't worry, Mrs. Blaze. You're not the first and likely won't be the last."

Red glanced at his wife and was surprised to find she was blushing. "What was all that about?" he asked.

"Just a little joke between us," replied Sue. "Isn't that the Akins' wagon outside Hacker's Store?"

She was afterwards pleased she'd managed to take Red's mind off what the doctor said to her. Red looked along the street to the small wagon with a pair of good horses which stood before Hacker Bland's General Store.

"That's them all right," he answered with a grin. "I'd take money old Hacker wishes it wasn't."

Sue grinned also. Mrs. Akins, full of pomp and dignity gained in Boston, was always a difficult customer for the owner of the store to deal with. Then Sue caught Red's arm and pointed ahead. A sudden fear came to her as she saw the group of men who lounged on the porch before the Apache Agency.

Five men stood on the porch, an oddly assorted group but one which could be seen here most days. Burton Hillvers, the Agent, was in the center of the group. He was that kind of man, always at the center of everything. A tall, florid, heavily built man who might have been handsome if one was partial to heavy moustaches, side whiskers, hair slicked down with bayrum and parted in the middle. He had his coat off, his shirt was a salmon pink color and his sleeve bands were multihued almost to the standard of Red's bandana. A heavy gold watch chain crossed his vest. His trousers were eastern style and his boots gleamed even with a thin coating of dust on them.

The other men were Gren, the county sheriff, a burly, unshaven man who was running to fat although still powerful. His clothes were just too good for the salary of a sheriff in a small and not rich county. His gunbelt hung right and the Smith and Wesson Russian model .44 in the holster was a fancy gun. Sharpe, a thin, moustached and untidy hardcase who hailed from Kansas, was the second man, on his vest the star of a deputy sheriff. His gunbelt supported two walnut handled Colt Civilian Peacemakers and he was said to be fast with them. The third of the group was a stocky, dirty and evil looking half-breed called No-Nose, dressed as always in dirty buckskins, with a Cavalry Colt in a half-breed holster, the top of the barrel emerging from the holster bottom which was not tied down. At the other side was a saw-edged bowie knife which Red regarded as an affectation. He was Hillver's interpreter, or supposed to be, for he was the result of a casual liaison between a bad white and a Ute squaw. Red felt the hair on the back of his neck rise as he thought of the tribe which gave No-Nose his name. Johnny Raybold had been shot by a Ute arrow. No-Nose's name was descriptive, for he'd lost most of his nasal organ in a knife fight and it did not improve his looks any.

The other two were gunmen pure and simple, hired toughs who sold their guns to the highest bidder and stayed on as long as the pay lasted. One was Turk, a big, lean man, not too bright or heroic although he could handle himself in a roughhouse or a shooting match pro-vided the opposition was not too high. The other looked out of place in such a crowd. He was a tall, slim and freshfaced boy in dandy cowhand dress of a cheaper kind. He had a brace of imitation pearl handled guns which he was apt to flash in what he fondly believed to be fast draws when the situation demanded it, or even when it did not if there was an appreciative audience. He was Boy Culver and took pay for his guns although he would have been hard put to justify his right to the pay against a real good man.

They made a hard looking group and there was little friendliness in their faces as they watched the buggy come to a halt and Red climb out. Sue followed her husband, hoping she would hold down his hot temper, for he was outnumbered. Hillvers said something in a low voice and Boy Culver laughed, loosening his Colts, a gesture he was very fond of making.

"Good day, Mrs. Blaze," Hillvers said, removing the thick black cigar from his mouth. "We don't often see you in town."

"Don't get in much," Sue replied. She'd never been able to take a liking to Hillvers although he was always polite and gentlemanly around her.

The other men moved off the porch, glancing at the wagon. Boy Culver's face was forming in a scowl. He knew he did not bluff or scare Red and the knowledge annoyed him. His eyes went to Sue who was wearing her frock again, the young woman looked straight through him and that also hurt, for he fancied his charm with women.

"Having any trouble out your way, Red?" Gren asked.

"Should I be?"

"I don't know. Colonel Akins allows he's been losing stock to the Apaches."

"We've lost none, but all our crew knows cattle work," Red answered. "Somebody took a shot at Hunting Wolf's gal on my land yesterday."

The faces of the men around Red did not change. Gren grinned and replied, "What'd she be doing coming on to your land?"

"Told me she was coming to town to ask why the supplies had been cut for the reservation."

"So the Apaches aren't getting their supplies now."

Hillver spoke gently, his eyes hard and his left hand tapping the seam of his trousers.

"That's what she said, her and Hunting Wolf both."

"And you believe him?"

"An Apache don't lie, a chief less than most," Red replied. "He said he got but half of what he should have."

"You're not trying to tell me my business, are you?"

Hillvers asked, and there was menace in his voice. "I'm in charge of the Agency."

"I know it," agreed Red. "And as far as I know you've never been out to the reservation and couldn't tell the difference between an Apache and a Sioux."

Hillver's face showed anger, the cheeks reddened, for he was strangely touchy about his lack of Indian knowledge. "What do you mean by that?"

"I've seen Apaches on the warpath and I'm not standing by while the Lipans are forced on to it."

"Is anyone trying to force them?" Hillvers asked, the rasp growing in his voice and causing Sue to glance to where Red's Spencer leaned against the wagon seat.

"They could be," Red replied, his eyes going to Culver. The young gunman stood with his hands resting on the butts of his guns. "Move your hands or I'll take those guns from you and ram them down your throat."

Two pairs of eyes locked, but it was Culver who looked away first. His eyes dropped from Red's and his hands came clear of his guns. He hated Red Blaze more than ever now, for he had been shamed, put down and made back water before a pretty young woman and his friends.

"You said Nogana's horse was killed—" Hillvers began.

"I didn't. But that's what happened. And somebody put a Ute arrow into my pard, Johnny Raybold. A *Ute* arrow." Gren moved forward, his face cold and angry. "There's no call for you to come here talking sassy and accusing folks—"

"Call off your tame lawdog, Hillvers," Red warned. "Or I'll kennel him with a Justin boot."

"He's real tough, boss, ain't he?" asked Sharpe, forgetting he was a public servant and not working for Hillvers.

No-Nose started to move forward and Red swung his right hand, knotted into a hard fist. The half-breed's nose was always a tender spot and the rock hard fist which smashed into it sent waves of pure agony through its owner. No-Nose spun around, reeling backwards, his hands clawing at his face, staggered to the wagon and crashed down on to his face, writhing in agony.

"Look out, Red!"

Sue's screamed warning came an instant too late. Sharpe lunged in behind Red, locking powerful arms around him, pinning his own arms to his sides. With a grin Turk swung a fist which smashed into Red's face, snapping his head to one side. Gren lashed a backhand slap at the same moment rocking Red's head back again.

It was then Sue forgot her worries about the baby which might be coming. Red, her husband, was in trouble and nothing else mattered. She turned and ran for the wagon and the Spencer. With that in her hands she would make the attackers hunt for cover. Sue's hands were almost on the butt of his rifle when Boy Culver grabbed her from behind, hauling her away. He locked his arms around her, holding down her strong arms with their hard little fists, then turned her to face her husband.

"Look at him, blonde gal," he sneered. "You won't recognize him when the boys have done with him."

Sue struggled desperately to get free, gasping, trying to do anything at all as the fists smashed into Red's face and body.

The batwing doors of the Apache City saloon opened and a small man stepped out. He was a cowhand, a Texas cowhand or the signs lied. On his head was a black J. B. Stetson, low crowned and wide brimmed, in the Texas style. Knotted around his throat was his bandana, tight rolled, long ends hanging down over his blue shirt. Around his waist was a brown leather buscadero gunbelt with a brace of white handled Colt Civilian Peacemakers butt forwards in the holsters. It looked strangely out of keeping with so small and insignificant a man.

The small Texan looked along towards the Indian Agency and the relaxed, leisurely look left him. He turned, snapped two words over his shoulder, then started along the sidewalk at a run, making for where Sharpe still held Red Blaze for the other two men to hit.

So engrossed in what they were doing were the men that they did not hear or see the small Texan coming until he was almost on them. Sharpe saw him first and yelled a warning. Gren started to turn, he was nearest to the sidewalk, his hand dropping to the butt of his gun. The small Texan leapt into the air, coming straight at Gren. Still in mid-air he drew his feet up, bending his knees, then straightening them again. The legs drove out straight, the high heeled boots aimed directly at Gren. One smashed full in the center of Gren's chest, the other drove with the power of a knob-head mule's kick into the middle of Gren's face. Gren went reeling backwards, his mouth smashed and bloody, pain whirling through his head. His fancy Smith and Wesson fell from his holster into the dirt at his feet as he went down.

The small Texan landed on his feet at the completion of the kick and Turk turned to attack him. It was a fine sentiment, this loyalty to one's friends and one which was foreign to Turk usually; but the Texan was small, not more than five foot six at most.

Turk hurled forward, his hands reaching for the cow-hand, meaning to crush him down by sheer strength. The Texan's left hand shot up, catching Turk's right wrist and heaving him off balance. At the same moment the Texan's right hand went between Turk's legs, his right leg slid along the ground and the left knee bent. Turk gave a yell as he was dragged across the Texan's shoulders. Bending his legs the small Texan got the gunman on his shoulders. Sharpe released Red Blaze, who sank to his hands and knees. Sharpe lunged forward, meaning to get the Texan and fix him good. With a strength that looked out of keeping for so small a man the Texan came up, straightening his legs and throwing Turk full at Sharpe, sending them both crashing down in a tangle of arms and legs.

Boy Culver released Sue, pushing her to one side, his hand going to the butt of his right side Colt, his eyes glowing with a lust to kill.

"Dusty!" Sue screamed.

The small Texan came around faster than a greased burned cat leaving a hot stove. His left hand moved in a flickering blur, the white handled Colt came from the holster at his right side, hammer drawing back under his thumb. It lined even as Culver's gun was sliding clear, flame lashed from the four and three-quarter inch blued barrel, smoke rolled. Culver screamed, spun around, throwing his gun to one side. By accident or by aim the .45 bullet from the small Texan's gun had caught Culver in the leg, right on the knee-cap and sent him down, a cripple for the rest of his life.

The Texan came around, his smoking Colt slanting at Turk and Sharpe who were untangling themselves and reaching hipwards. At the sight of that gun they froze solid and fast. Small he might be but the Texan was one of the real fast guns. That showed in the way he'd drawn and cut down Boy Culver. A man did not take any chances with such a fast gun—not twice at any rate.

For all that the small Texan had made a bad error in tactics. To one side Gren was fumbling his hand towards the butt of his Smith and Wesson, and by the buggy No-Nose was on his knees, bloody face twisted in almost maniacal rage as he gripped the butt of his revolver. The small Texan was boxed, whipsawed and would soon be nothing more dangerous than a marker in the town's boothill.

Hillver watched all this. He never became involved in anything dangerous if he could avoid it. His eyes went to the small Texan who should soon be dead.

The Stetson was hanging back by its storm strap and the Texan's hair was a dusty blond color. His face was tanned, handsome, a strong face with grey eyes that were firm, hard and decisive and a jaw which showed more strength than was warranted by so insignificant a man. His clothing was good quality, his hat and boots costly and that gunbelt bore the stamp of a master leather-worker. It was strange that so small a man should have such a belt.

Sue Blaze was by her husband, kneeling and trying to roll him over. The small man looked down at her and asked, without relaxing his aim on Sharpe and Turk, "Is he all right, Sue gal?"

It was at that moment Gren gripped the butt of his gun. His fingers closed around it ready to sweep it up and fire. A boot with a high heel came driving down. The heel smashed down on to Gren's hand, pinning it to the ground like a nail through wood. Gren let out an agonized scream of pain, his fingers opened. Then fingers like steel clamps gripped, sinking into the flab of Gren's neck and hauling him to his feet. Gren then caught a backhand slap which rocked his head, smashed his already bloody lips and sent him crashing into the hitching rail.

Gren's attacker was a tall man, even in this land of tall men. Full three and more inches over six foot he stood, his white, costly Stetson with its silver concha decorated band doing nothing to lessen his giant size. His hair was golden blond, his face as handsome as that of a classic Greek god of old. His costly, made-to-measure tan shirt covered a great spread of shoulders, a lean waist and arms which were muscled like a giant of mythology. Yet for all that the handsome giant did not move or look slow and that gunbelt with the low tied, ivory handled Colt Cavalry Peacemakers was no decoration. It was the rig of a real fast man who knew how to handle his guns.

Studying the Texan, mad with pain, Gren made a foolish mistake. He pushed himself from the hitching rail and swung a punch which had weight and muscle but little else to commend it. The big blond deflected the fist with a casual flip of his right hand. The left fist drove out and sank almost wrist deep into Gren's stomach. It was a beautiful punch, thrown with skill and landing right on the spot where it would do most good or harm, depending on which end of the blow one was. Gren croaked in agony, his life over the past months did not fit him for taking blows like that. He doubled over and the Texan's right fist came down, then drove up. There was a click like two billiard balls meeting and Gren snapped erect. He went backwards, smashed into the hitching rail, traveling with speed enough to break the stout bar, then he crashed on to the sidewalk and lay still.

While this was happening No-Nose found he'd troubles of his own. With the gun almost clear of leather he heard a soft footfall behind him, then a boot smashed full into the center of his back and sent him sprawling face down again, writhing in more agony. Snarling curses in the Ute and English No-Nose rolled over, the gun had gone but he was reaching for his knife when he saw his attacker. Then there was not enough money in the world for him to chance drawing the weapon.

He stood with legs apart; an innocent looking almost babyishly handsome, lean, lithe and tall youngster. His face was dark, almost Indian-dark but his eyes were red-hazel in color, cold and dangerous. His clothing was all black, from hat through bandana, shirt, levis to boots there was no other color. Even the leather of his gunbelt was black, the blackness being relieved briefly by the walnut grips of the old Second Model Dragoon Colt which was butt forward at his right side, balancing the empty knife sheath at his left. The knife, a genuine James Black bowie, was not in the sheath. The dark faced boy gripped the eleven and a half inch long, two and a half inch wide blade in his right hand, holding it casually by his side. Too casually. No-Nose boasted of being a knife fighting man and he knew a master when he saw one. He knew the knife was not held in such a manner by any accident or because the dark youngster was trying to be cute. It was held ready to be whipped up and thrown.

"Try it *hombre!*" said the dark boy, his voice a pleasant, untrained tenor yet with the harder, colder grunt of a Comanche Dog Soldier in it. "Just try and take it out."

No-Nose was staring, his memory going back a few years to a town on the Rio Grande and a baby-faced, innocent-looking boy who wore all black clothing and was armed as this one here. The name of that boy came back to No-Nose and he croaked it out in a strangled and fear-filled gasp.

"The Ysabel Kid!"

Hillvers had been debating what action he should take until he heard that name. Heard it and knew it. Knew also the name of the blond giant and the small, insignificant Texan.

"The Ysabel Kid?" gasped Sharpe, getting to his feet, his eyes on the small Texan. "Then you're—"

"That's right, you yellow rat, Sharpe," Sue Blaze hissed as her husband tried to push her away and make his feet. "He's Dusty Fog."

Which put a different complexion on matters and altered any unborn ideas Sharpe and Turk might have had about resuming hostilities.

Dusty Fog. The name was spoken from one end of the West to the other end and far beyond. It was told that he'd been a Confederate Army captain at seventeen and a cavalry leader whose skill ranked with John Singleton Mosby or Turner Ashby, the greats of the Confederate cavalry. Men told how Dusty Fog brought law to at least two wild and wide open towns when lesser men died in the trying.* How he was a trail boss with a name second only to the old trail drive master John Chisholm himself. He was talked of as a horse tamer as good as could be found. Of how he was the segundo of the biggest ranch in Texas, Ole Devil Hardin's O.D. Connected, leader of the elite of the ranch crew, Ole Devil's floating outfit, two members of which were along with him. They said Dusty Fog knew some strange fighting

*Told in: *Quiet Town, The Town Tamers, The Trouble Busters* and *The Making of a Law Man.*

tricks, learned from his uncle's Japanese servant, that enabled him to whip bigger, stronger men. They said also he was a master with his bone-handled Colts, and no man was his peer in the art of draw and shoot. Whatever they said, no matter how unlikely it might appear on first look at the small, insignificant man they called Dusty Fog, it was all true.

Mark Counter, the handsome blond giant even now blowing on his right knuckles as he looked at the unconscious lawman, was Dusty's right hand man. If anything Mark was better with cattle than was Dusty. He had been the Beau Brummel of Bushford Sheldon's Confederate Cavalry and now was the acknowledged arbiter of cowhand dress. What Mark Counter wore today was likely to be worn in copy by cowhands from one end of the range to the other. There was more than just a dandy dresser to Mark though. His strength was a legend, his fist fighting prowess having barely been put to test right here. He was known to be a good shot with a rifle but his skill with his matched Colts was but little known, for he rode in the shadow of Dusty Fog.

The last of that trio, standing ready, willing and more than able to throw and sink his bowie knife into the chest of No-Nose, was the Ysabel Kid. There were many legends spun about this innocent looking boy down on the Rio Grande. The border Mexicans told tales of his uncanny skill with a rifle, first a Mississippi and currently with the Model of 1873 Winchester in the saddleboot of his white stallion which, with the mounts of his two friends was standing in the shade around the side of the saloon. They told how the Kid's father had been a wild Irish-Kentuckian and his mother a French Creole-Comanche girl, daughter of Chief Long Walker of the Dog Soldier lodge. They told how the Kid could move in the silence of a ghost, follow the tracks of man or beast, old or fresh laid. They said he could speak six Indian languages and fluent Spanish. That he could handle his knife in the manner of the old Texas master Colonel James Bowie. Whatever they said it all added to one small thing. The Ysabel Kid was a good friend, a real bad enemy and one who would not hesitate to send the knife forward into human flesh.

There were few people on the street now, for the citizens of Apache City had early learned not to show too much curiosity at the doings of Burton Hillvers and his men.

Red Blaze forced himself to his feet, blood running from his nose and lips, right eye swelling. Sue supported his weight as he got his breath back and looked at Hillvers.

"Feel like doing your own fighting, Hillvers?" he gasped.

Mark Counter moved by, giving Sue a warm and friendly smile. His eyes went to Hillvers' face and he said, "You set back and let me have him for you, Red boy."

Hillvers backed off a pace or two, his face lost some of its color. He was a fair man in a fight, but the blond giant was better than fair. The easy way he'd handled Gren proved that and Hillvers did not want the same treatment.

"Yellow as they make 'em," Sue snapped, her blue eyes showing her hate and loathing. "Don't hit him, Mark. He's not got the guts of a jackrabbit."

Red pushed from his wife and stood swaying. Through his puffed up lips he growled a warning.

"Get this and get it good, Hillvers. I'm going to see the next supplies that go out to the reservation and I'm making sure they agree with what the treaty promised. If it's wrong I'll start a stink that'll get to the Governor and make him take action."

Hillvers got some of his color back. His hands clenched and the cigar was crushed between his fingers.

"I'll remember," he answered.

"And if I see that breed riding my range with either a Sharps rifle or a bow I'll drop him on sight."

Hillvers looked to where No-Nose was still on the ground, cowering before the menacing black dressed shape of the Ysabel Kid. The bowie knife flipped into the air, was caught and thrust back into its sheath once more and the Kid looked down at No-Nose, then in what the half-breed admitted was better than fair Ute, gave out a warning.

"What Red says goes double for me—and I'll be around for a spell."

"Get in your wagon, Cousin Red," said the small man called Dusty Fog. "Go where you're going. We'll follow along."

Sue did not give her husband time to argue. She started his feet moving towards the wagon and Red obeyed her. He swung into the seat, she went round the other side, caught the wink the Kid gave her and climbed in to take up the reins.

"We'll be down at the store, Dusty," she said.

CHAPTER FOUR

Comanche Blake's Girl

Sue smiled at the three men but her eyes were on the smallest of the three, the Rio Hondo gun wizard, Dusty Fog. He apparently thought that some explanation of their presence in Apache County was needed.

"Uncle Devil sent us along to see if you pair had got some sense whomped into your heads by Johnny and Red."

"They knocked some into us," Red put in, forcing himself to his feet and out of the wagon. "You boys never showed up at a better time."

"Like I said, Uncle Devil sent us," Dusty answered. "Figured it'd be time when you need some more hands to help make a good round-up. Waco and Doc's coming along in a few days with that bunch of blood horses you said you'd graze for us."

Red and Sue exchanged glances. It was typical of the hard eyed old man who ruled the mighty O.D. Connected cattle empire that he would send his segundo and the full floating outfit to help the S-B ranch make a start. To hire men for a round-up would take more money than the ranch could easily spare, now they had three good hands with two more coming along. The round-up of the S-B range could be made with every chance of success.

"You three are bad enough," Sue snorted. "But Doc Leroy and Waco too! How did you get Waco to stay behind while you came on?"

"Tied him down, told Doc to shoot him in the leg if he cut loose after us," Mark answered. "You get prettier every time I see you, Sue honey. I told you that you should have married me."

Dusty watched the others with a smile on his face.

"Come on in the store," Sue suggested. "Only don't act like you're with us. I don't want ruining socially."

"I bet you'll chance it if there's any heavy toting to be done," drawled the Kid.

"Somebody'll have to do it," Red replied. "I'm all stove up and can't."

Dusty glanced at his cousin, then looked back along the street to the Agency where Sharpe and Turk were carrying Culver inside the building and No-Nose was coming from the door carrying a bucket of water to try and get Gren back on his feet. Better than any man, better possibly than Sue even, Dusty knew his cousin Red, knew his way of getting into fights. There was more than just a chance insult behind the beating though, Dusty was sure of that. The talk between Red and the big dude meant nothing yet, but this was not the time to ask about it.

The others followed the Blaze family into the general

store. General was the correct term, for inside the large building a man could buy almost anything he would need to live in the West.

Sue took one of Bland's chairs and Red sank willingly into the other. "You all right, honey?" she asked.

"I'll make do," he answered. "There's nothing broken."

"You didn't give them enough time," Dusty put in. "What was it all about, Cousin Red?"

Red told Dusty all that had happened the previous day and sketched the situation in Apache County. For all the expression any of the other three men showed he might have been discussing the weather, but he knew they were all listening and real interested.

Hacker Bland came across the room, as usual he wore an apron over his vest, white shirt, tie and black trousers. He was a thin man, pallid and given to coughing fits. He'd come West to die of a disease, that was ten years back and although he would never admit to feeling well he was still running his store, doing all his own heavy lifting and spent a good part of every night at the Apache Saloon playing poker to his own profit. He went to the Apache City post office, a large wooden box at the rear end of the room, beyond which was a telegraph sending and receiving tapper. Taking out a pile of letters he started back and halted by the Blaze family.

"Howdy, Sue, Red," he greeted, glancing at the marks on Red's face. Rangewise he asked no questions. "How're you keeping?"

"Well enough. Johnny met with an accident, but he's all right now," Sue replied. "And don't look at me, I didn't do it to Red."

"Thought maybe you had," grunted Hacker, then glanced to where Dusty and the Kid were glancing through the latest copy of the *Police Gazette* to reach Apache City. "Friends of yours?"

Red shook his head. "Not of mine. Some of Sue's poor kin."

Sue gave a squeak of protest. "They're not my kin, thank you 'most to death. That's Dusty Fog, Mark Counter and the Ysabel Kid. I'd bet they've come to rob the bank or something."

Hacker grinned at the girl, wondering if she was jobbing him. He knew cowhands, could read the signs and knew that here were three tophands of their craft. He'd seen enough of fast guns to know a pair of the best when he saw them. They could be the men named and that dark boy did look like the Ysabel Kid.

"I never heard of those three robbing anyone," he pointed out.

"They've robbed every cook they've ever come across," snorted Sue and called the three Texans over to be introduced.

From the beam of delight on Hacker's face he might have been introduced to royalty, or to President Grant himself. He shook hands with the three men, then Red asked:

"Did you see what Hillvers sent out to the reservation, Hacker?"

"Sure. Me and Hoe were playing checkers out front when the wagon went by and the stock. We counted them and looked it over. Hunting Wolf's too good a customer for us to want to lose his trade. The wagon was loaded like always and there was the usual thirty head of prime beef."

"Which same never reached the reservation," Red growled. "Or so Hunting Wolf told me yesterday and I don't reckon he lied."

"Nor more do I," Hacker answered.

He was a worried man, for he'd been through Indian wars before and knew what it meant. This time it would be far worse, for the Lipans had fought with the cavalry as scouts and knew the tactics of the soldiers.

"Mr. Bland, I really can't wait all day!"

A severe looking woman had turned and spoken, her voice straight from the better part of Boston. She stood glowering towards the storekeeper, ignoring Red, Sue and the others as if they were not there at all. Her two daughters were standing to one side and trying on Stetson hats without much success. Sue watched them and thought she could show them how to set the hats right on their heads but made no attempt to do so. Bland walked away from the counter towards his other customers and the three Texans were about to go back to their study of the *Police Gazette* when the store door bell clanged and another customer came in.

She was a tall girl, six inches taller than Sue at least. Her hair was shoulder long, held back by a blue silk band and red as the coat of a deer. Her face had a rich golden tan; it was a beautiful face, wild, untamed and reckless. She had a fringed buckskin shirt which emphasized the rich swell of her full breasts. Her slim waist had a broad silver concha decorated belt around it and a Comanche scalping knife was sheathed at her right side. The jeans she wore were tight and showed the curve of her hips and the hard, shapely power of her thighs. Hanging outside her boots cowhand style the jeans had the cuffs turned back. She moved with a long legged, free-striding grace far removed from the undulating sway of a dancehall girl, yet with the full implied impact of one.

For a moment the girl stood at the door, looking around the room with an alert caution. Then she smiled and came forward towards the Blaze family.

"Hi Sue, Red," she said, her voice rather deep, husky yet attractive. "How're you keeping. I haven't seen you for near on a week. Thought you'd gone all high-tone and stand-offish."

The *Police Gazette* suddenly lost all its attraction to Dusty Fog, Mark Counter and the Ysabel Kid. They stood up straighter and their hats came sweeping from their heads. Sue smiled, kept them writhing for a moment, then turned to the girl.

"Comanche, meet one of my poor kin and two of his worthless *amigos*. They're not worth a cuss alone or in a bunch. This's Dusty Fog, Mark Counter and the Ysabel Kid. Boys, meet Comanche Blake."

The girl who was known as Comanche Blake flashed a glance at Sue, half suspecting a joke. She knew Red Blaze was kin to Dusty Fog but could not at first see this small man as being him. Then she got the full measure of Dusty's appearance, for Comanche knew cowhands. Her eyes flickered to Mark's great spread of shoulders, took in his handsome face and could see that he possibly was who Sue claimed. Then she looked at the Kid and their eyes held each others. Her hand reached out to him and she knew a certain way to prove or disprove Sue's statement.

"You are the grandson of Long Walker, old man chief of the Dog Soldier lodge," she said, the guttural Comanche flowing easily from her tongue.

"I am, Fire Bird," the Kid replied, his voice holding the exact tone of a Dog Soldier. "Didn't you think I was?"

The Kid held her hand a moment longer than was necessary. He and she felt their alikeness, their wild spirit. The stirrings of their blood called to each other, for they were the same, wild, spirited and not likely to be hampered by self-restraint.

For all that Comanche could not bring her range-trained self to ask an obvious question of these three Texans. She could not ask them if they were staying in town, so swung her eyes back to Sue and asked:

"Will you be at the dance a week come Saturday?"

Sue smiled, knowing the question might be directed to her, but that it was meant for the Ysabel Kid.

"Likely," she said. "Unless my husband's shiftless kin and *amigos* haven't eaten us out of house and home."

"We'll be here, girl," Mark promised. "Just to show you what the New Mexican ladies have been missing."

"Which same won't be much from the look of you," scoffed Comanche Blake.

The Kid sensed the challenge to him in the words. "You come, gal," he drawled sardonically, "and I'll teach you how to dance the *paso doble*—happen I can find a gal in this one-hoss town who could partner me."

"You?" Comanche said. "That'll be the day."

"It surely will, ma'am," agreed Dusty. "Lon here dances like a one-legged Sioux at a coffin-varnish hoe-down."

"Waal, if he can dance at all I'll dance him until his legs are so short he'll need a long ladder to get on to his hoss."

Mark could see there was no chance of cutting in and so bowed out of trying. He turned and walked to where the two girls were still fooling with the Stetsons, looking at themselves in the mirror and trying to settle the hats on their heads.

"Allow me, ladies," he said, reaching out and taking the taller girl's hat. With deft fingers he altered the shape to something more Western, then placed it on her head again. "You have to get it just right, tilted forward like this over the off eye."

The girl looked at Mark, a smile flickering on her face.

"Come, my dears!" The severe-looking woman's voice held a sour rasp of disapproval. "We must be getting back home."

"Could we take the hats, mama?" asked the little blonde.

"Very well, put them on the account, Mr. Bland."

There was a large box of supplies on the counter and Mark stepped forward with a polite bow. He picked up the box and carried it outside, setting it in the wagon, then glancing at the brand the team carried.

"Lazy D, now who'd own that brand?" he asked.

"My father, Colonel Akins," answered the blonde.

"Celia, my dear," Mrs. Akins climbed into the wagon, "Your papa will be annoyed if we are late returning home."

With a look of disappointment the blonde girl climbed up beside her mother, Mark handed the other girl up and stepped back. Mrs. Akins clucked to the team and Mark heard her say, "Really, girls, I'm surprised at you. Talking to a common cowhand like that."

Celia looked back, shoving her Stetson on firmer. This was the sort of man she always dreamed about.

Mark grinned. His father owned a ranch the size of Apache County and he himself had a bank account which would be as large as Colonel Akins, due to a legacy left by an eccentric aunt when she died. He could have settled down and bought a spread of his own, but much preferred to ride with his friends as a member of the Ole Devil Hardin's floating outfit.

"Damned high-toned ole goat."

Mark turned to find Hacker Bland standing by him.

"Who is she?"

"Colonel Akins' missus. Born, raised and lived in Boston and ought to have stopped there."

"Two nice looking gals though."

"Yeah," agreed Hacker dryly. "That young Captain van Sillen up at the fort, he reckons so, too. Reckons it real hard with Miss Amanda, the oldest. Akins is one of the County Commissioners and van Sillen's a regular caller at the house."

"He as good looking as me?" asked Mark with a grin.

"Couldn't be wuss looking. Thanks for selling me those hats. The gals have been at them every time they come in but wouldn't take them. I'd best get in and attend to my business afore I lose customers."

"Where'd they go?"

Mark stood on the sidewalk studying the town. There were a couple of new business premises on the street but most of the others had been running for years. There was the ubiquitous Wells Fargo office further along the street and all the other things a man expected to see in such a town. His eyes went to the horse which was standing at the hitching rail next to the wagon. It was a short coupled, speedy looking roan with a wicked look in its eye. The saddle was a double girth rig and in the saddleboot, the butt handy for gripping, was a short Winchester Model 1873 carbine. That would be Comanche Blake's horse, it looked almost as wild and spirited as the girl herself.

The sight of the horse reminded Mark and he stepped from the sidewalk to make for the saloon. That there were several men in town who had cause to hate him did not worry Mark. He was confident he could handle the play of any of that bunch they tangled with earlier. He went along to the side of the saloon and collected the four horses which were standing hipshot in the shade. He loosed the reins of his big bloodbay stallion and Dusty's seventeen hand paint, then released the packpony which carried their warbags and bedrolls. The Kid's big, magnificent looking white stallion stood free, it never needed fastening. Mark did not touch that big white, it was not safe to take too many liberties with the horse. However, when he started towards the store leading his bloodbay, the paint and the packpony, the white followed on his heels like a well trained hound dog.

Red came from the store followed by Dusty and the Kid who were carrying a box of supplies each. Comanche Blake and Sue followed them, the girl had a small sack in her hands, she went to the roan and lashed the sack to the saddlehorn and unfastened the reins.

"I should go down there and talk real formal with Hillvers," Red said grimly.

"No you don't, redtop!" Sue snapped. "He's not going any place and he'll watch what he's doing now. Get in the wagon."

Dusty looked along the street. He had expected the woman and her daughters to be waiting outside to talk gossip with Sue and Comanche. There was no sign of them and he looked towards Sue.

"What's wrong with folks hereabouts. They don't act friendly at all."

"They don't cotton none to us," Sue replied. "I always reckon anybody who doesn't want my company needn't have it."

"See, Dusty, when we heard about this place and I came down here I didn't know Colonel Akins brought a bunch of folks out here aiming to settle the county. He wanted all the spreads to belong to folks he knew, but they arrived late. I'd bought the SB and Comanche the

Stirrup Iron. It didn't set well with them."

"They making fuss with you?" asked Mark, tossing Dusty the paint's reins.

"Nope, they leave us alone and we do the same for them."

"Man'd think those folk'd be happy to have you around," remarked the Kid. "Them not knowing any better they might allow you know cattle; which same neither you nor Johnny do worth a cuss. They could have got some help from you."

"Well, they haven't," Sue snorted before Red could object to the Kid's words. "Johnny and Red tried to get them to join in with us but they wouldn't, so we just let them ride their own hosses."

"And they've made real bad mistakes all the way along," Red went on. "None of them know anything about cattle. Akins' foreman's a big Irishman, ran the Akins factory and tries the same games back here. He treats his hands mean and he doesn't know sic 'em about cattle."

"Got him a high-brown gal for a wife, real honey she is," Comanche Blake went on mildly. "She called me white-trash once—only the once though."

"Yeah," agreed Sue with a grin, for she remembered the incident.

Not until they were mounted and riding from town did Comanche mention anything she knew of the happenings of the previous day.

"I was out to the reservation early this morning, saw Nogana. She told me all that happened yesterday. I'm pleased you saved her, she's a good friend. If she'd have been killed Hunting Wolf would've painted for war and Shinqua wouldn't quit until every white man in the territory was staked out in the anthills. The rest of the Lipans would have followed. They're sick of being starved and cheated."

"Hacker allows the right supplies left here last time," Red pointed out.

"I was at the reservation. I know what arrived and it wasn't half of the allowance. I sent Dingle and Pike, them's my hands," Comanche answered, glancing at the newcomers, "with thirty head."

"That's a tolerable few head to give away," Dusty remarked.

"My west line runs on to Hillvers' spread, he runs it just over the county line. Ole Dingle and Pike picked up thirty head of his stock and took them over. One way or another Hillvers' going to feed the Lipans."

They rode along the wagon trail, leaving the town behind them. The talk was of the shooting of Nogana's horse and of Johnny Raybold. Dusty turned to the Kid and said:

"Allow you should head out there and cut for sign, Lon. See what you can make out about who did the shooting."

Comanche threw back her head and gave a wild peel of laughter. The Kid scowled at her. "What's so funny?"

"I never saw a Dog Soldier who could read sign worth a nickel," she scoffed. "Why I bet you couldn't follow a dragged log through sand unless you was real sure which way it was going."

"And I never saw a Fox Lodge squaw who was worth a wored out windbroke pony for a bride price," replied the Kid. "Happen anybody was fool enough to want one, that is."

"Whyn't you bring that wored out, windbroke bangtail

over and see?" she answered, looking defiantly at him.

The Kid grinned. If he took a bride price to Comanche Blake it would be better than any windbroke bangtail, that was for sure. Then the Kid stopped grinning. He'd never thought of any woman in those terms before.

Comanche was suddenly aware that they were approaching the place where her path would part from the Kid's. There were two trails branching off the one they were following, the right leading to her place, the left to the Akins' ranch. The rolling range hid any sight of the other wagon which did not surprise Comanche for the Akins family would not want her company. She decided she would go along to the S–B and could use Johnny's injury as an excuse.

Even as Comanche opened her mouth to make the excuse she heard something which drove all thought of excuses from her head. The others heard it also. The wild yells of Indians as they raced their war ponies into an attack. It came from the left and it only meant one thing.

Out there, hidden from sight by a fold in the land, a war party was either chasing or had caught up with the wagon and the three defenseless women who rode in it.

CHAPTER FIVE

The Kid Makes War

The hooves of the horses churned dust up as they came to a halt. Every eye looked towards the yells and screams. For an instant only did they stop, then Dusty was barking out his orders.

"Red, fort down here with that Spencer. Sue, here's my carbine. Let's go."

Sue caught the Winchester carbine Dusty tossed her, worked the lever and threw a bullet into the breech. Then four horses were heading toward the sounds. Four it was for Comanche Blake, riding astride and with the skill of the cowhands, was urging her roan after the others. The roan was a good horse, but it was not in the same class as the three big stallions and the girl found herself being left behind.

Dusty, Mark and the Kid came up to the head of the

slope and below saw that they were going to be close if
not too late. The wagon had come to a halt, one of its
horses dead. The Indians, squat, long haired, wearing
gaudy shirts, trade trousers and knee high moccasins,
were sweeping in to the attack. They looked like Apaches,
twenty of them in all.

On the wagon Amanda was showing she had the right
spirit, she was on her feet gripping the whip and her face
was set, determined. Her sister was standing by her just
as pale and determined, tiny hands held in fists. Their
mother crouched on the floor of the wagon, eyes dilated,
in a faint. The Indians were coming in, only two of them
held firearms and were not shooting. The others had
lances or bows and were not wasting their arrows. They
were coming in to count coup at best, commit rape and
murder at worst.

Dusty's hands crossed and his matched Colts were
out, the reins looped around his saddlehorn. By his side
Mark also held a gun in either hand and was setting the
spurs to his big stallion.

"Yeeah!"

The war yell of the Texas Light Cavalry shattered the
air and two, only two, horses hurled down the slope to
make a slashing attack on the rear of the Indians.

Comanche Blake could hardly believe her eyes when
she saw the Kid was not going with his friends. Hot
anger and shame filled her. She had listened to the war
yells with a cold and sinking feeling. Had Hunting Wolf's
braves finally grown tired of the indignities heaped on
them and taken up the war hatchet? Those thoughts went
as she saw that dark grandson of Chief Long Walker halt
his horse and let his two friends go down the slope into
a fight.

Comanche felt her eyes filling with tears as she raced

her horse to the Kid. The rifle came into the Kid's shoulder even as Comanche reached his side. Down below she saw why he'd come to a stop.

The wagon was surrounded by Indians, but they were keeping from the lashing bite of the whip. Not for long, one of them was already swinging an arrow on to his bow-string and another was raising his rifle.

The Winchester kicked back against the Kid's shoulder and the rifle toter spun around, his weapon falling from his hands as he pitched down. Before his body hit the ground the second brave was crumpling forward, his bow still not strung. It was mute testimony to the Kid's skill with his Winchester. The rifle was swinging and blasted once more to send a brave stumbling by the end of the wagon as he tried to get in close enough to use his knife on the women.

By this time Dusty and Mark were at the foot of the slope and the Kid could see there was no longer need for him to use his rifle. His big white stallion was standing like a statue and he raced forward to go into the saddle with a bound. The stallion was running down the slope even as the Kid landed and Comanche followed. She no longer felt ashamed of the Kid for stopping, seeing why he did it. Now she was following him into the fight, every wild Comanche spot of blood coursing through her.

Dusty Fog's matched Colts started to beat out their tattoo of death as he sent the huge paint hurling towards the attacking braves. By his side Mark was also shooting, throwing his lead fast and accurately.

The Indians turned, saw the smoke and flame spurting devils tearing at them. One man tossed aside his lance and pitched to his face. Another was about to cut loose with an arrow when he seemed to be struck by an invisible hand which threw him clean off his feet.

The Indians broke, those still on horses fleeing wildly, the ones who had dismounted racing and bounding on to their bangtail ponies. There were eight shapes on the ground, still and unmoving. Dusty and Mark did not stop their horses at the foot of the slope and by the wagon, but sent them on after the fleeing Indians.

The Kid and Comanche Blake reached the foot of the slope. The girl tore by the wagon, for she was not over-worried at the possible fate of Mrs. Akins and wanted to see where the raiders were going. There was a nagging doubt in Comanche's head, her Indian blood warned her there was something wrong. She could not think what exactly it was, but there was something that did not fit into the correct scheme of things.

Swinging down from his horse the Kid went towards the wagon where the girls were kneeling by their mother. He passed one of the still forms on the ground without a glance, for his eyes were on the girls. They had seen battle and sudden death for the first time but were bearing up under it well. So far the reaction had not set in and the Kid wanted to be on hand to help them if it did.

A hand gripped his ankle and he went sprawling down. He heard the scream Celia Akins let out even as he went down, twisting over to land on his back. One of the supposedly dead Indians was far from being so. Even now he was diving forward, his knife hand whipping up and driving down. The Kid twisted over fast, felt the wind of the knife as it passed him and sank into the sand. He went on rolling and came to his feet even as the Indian was up and attacking.

The Kid's fingers closed around the ivory hilt of the bowie knife and brought it from leather, the cutting edge held upwards in a hand that knew knife fighting from start to gory end. He crouched on the balls of his feet, eyes on the knife in the hand of the Apache. He heard Celia scream again, saw she was pointing behind him, saw it from the corner of his eye, for he could spare none of his attention from the attacking brave.

Behind the Kid a second Indian was struggling to his knees. He was wounded and must have been stunned by going down. Now he was recovered and ready to cut in. He had the bow in his hands, an arrow on the string and was drawing it back.

Comanche Blake had turned to look back at the first scream from the wagon. What she saw brought her horse in a tight turn which would have seen a lesser rider ploughing dirt with her chin. Comanche rode the turn with the ease of her mother, a squaw from the finest horse-Indians of them all. She sent the horse leaping forward to help her man, for that was how Comanche Blake now thought of the Ysabel Kid. Comanche did not scream or point in her efforts to help. She was a western woman and her help was completely practical. The scalping knife, with an edge sharper than many a barber's razor and a point set exactly in the center of the blade for throwing accuracy, slid into her hand. Her right arm whipped back even as the bow was drawn almost to its fullest and the arrow lined ready to fly into white flesh. The arm lashed down, the knife made a flicker of light in the sun, then the flicker merged with the gaudy trade shirt of the Indian. He arched his back, the arrow jerked loose, snapped off harmlessly to land at his feet. He started to make his feet but the shoulder of Comanche's horse caught him and flung him sprawling on to his face. He struggled weakly, almost made himself get on to hands and knees, then fell forward on to his face.

The Kid may or may not have heard what was hap-

pening behind him. He saw the Indian leap forward, saw
the knife ripping at him and moved with the speed of his
Comanche forefathers. The bowie knife deflected the
other blade, sent it harmlessly by him, then he thrust,
the razor edge ripping out. The Indian had struck at a
white man and expected no trouble. The reply came not
from a white man but from a Comanche and there was
no beter man with a knife than such a warrior. Desperately the Indian tried to stop himself going forward but
it was too late. His entire weight had been thrown into
the blow and now it missed he was out of control. The
bowie knife's great blade slashed underneath the Indian's
guard, bit through the shirt and deep into the stomach
below. Down through flesh it sank, the blood spurting
out over the Kid's hand and the hot rush of stomach
gases blowing on to him. Up ripped the knife and the
Ysabel Kid stepped back. The blade of the bowie was
red from end to end and the Indian crumpled forward to
crash down on to his face. From the wampum belt around
the middle of the dead brave three scalps fell, the scalps
of white men, for no Indian ever had blond, auburn or
brown hair.

Then it was over and the reaction gripped the two
Akins girls. Celia gave a scream and covered her face,
sinking on to the seat while Amanda's legs gave way
and she sank down beside her mother, trying to tear her
eyes away from that bloody thing which lay before her.

Comanche Blake showed no such feminine traits as
she swung down from her horse. She bent over her victim
and pulled the knife out, cleaned the blade on his shirt,
then sheathed it and looked to where the Kid was cleaning
his bowie knife.

"You all right?" she asked.

"Sure, gal," replied the Kid and looked down at the

still writhing form at his feet. "I never knew Apaches to pull a trick like that."

Comanche nodded. The brave had been unwounded and had feigned death to take a chance on getting at least one coup on the white folks. A smart trick, a brave trick, but not the trick any Apache would play.

"Easy Celia, gal," Comanche said, turning to the wagon and putting a hand on the younger girl's arm. "It had to be done, now stop this fussing."

Celia's sobs came to an end, she turned a pale and frightened face to Comanche Blake. Amanda was also looking, her face pallid, but she seemed to be getting fast control of her nerves. Her eyes went to her mother who still lay in the faint.

"Do something," gasped Amanda.

"A pleasure," grinned Comanche.

There was a large canteen of water in the wagon and Comanche took it up, opening the lid and leaning over.

"That's our drinking water," Amanda protested.

"Shucks, there's three good clean springs on the way to your place, even if it was far enough for you to need water."

With that Comanche poured the water from the canteen over Mrs. Akins' face. The woman gasped, her eyes came open. There was fear in them and she managed to push herself into a sitting position, staring wildly around her.

"Don't look out here!"

Comanche gave a grim warning and luckily Mrs. Akins did as the girl said, for the shapes around the wagon were not a pretty sight. She heard horses aproaching and guessed from the lack of concern the others showed that friends were on hand.

Dusty and Mark came back, bringing their horses to

a halt. Comanche flashed them a grin, then her eyes went to the scalps which lay beside the victim of the Kid's bowie knife. She opened her mouth to say something about this and saw that Dusty was also looking down at them. He caught her eye and shook his head gently.

"These gentlemen saved us from the Apaches, mama," Amanda told her mother.

The Kid and Comanche both opened their mouths but once more Dusty shook his head. Comanche frowned but the Kid looked hard at her and shook his head in a grim warning. The girl gave a snort and turned her attention to Dusty once more.

Mrs. Akins stared at the Texans, opened her mouth to say something but did not know how to word her thanks correctly. She knew little of the west, but knew that cowhands did not take kindly to any form of patronage.

"Let's get this wagon away from here," Dusty ordered.

That presented something of a problem, for one of the two-horse team was dead and the other would not be able to pull the heavy wagon. To try and harness any of their horses would not be a great success, for they would never accept such an indignity. The packhorse, tied to Red's wagon now, would be no better, for it had never been broken to harness.

The problem of the wagon was temporarily shelved by Mark's pointed finger and his growl of, "Company, Dusty!"

The other turned and saw dust rolling up over the slope beyond them. Dusty glanced at the Kid, who shook his head.

"Not Injun raisings," he said. "Soldiers I'd reckon, or cowhands."

The men who came over the rim were blue-coated cavalry, a tall, smart looking young officer in the lead. From his appearance he was a career officer with money behind him and possibly some influence in high places, for he was young to have the three bars of a captain, especially a captain on frontier duty. His uniform was well cut, smart and more usual in Washington or some Eastern garrison than out on the plains. The men behind him were young, with one exception, and gave the impression of being recruits left at a safe outpost to learn duties before being shipped west. The exception was the troop sergeant, a lean, tanned and hard looking man who alone wore a campaign hat. There was something familiar about him, something in the way he sat a horse which Dusty remembered.

Down the slope came the men, a full dozen of them riding in pairs behind the captain and his sergeant, and following the guidon carrier.

Halting smartly, van Sillen looked down at the bodies, at the women in the wagon, then at the three Texans and the cold eyed, unsmiling girl who stood with them. He jerked his gauntlets off and slapped them hard against the striped leg of his trousers.

"To think I was just talking to Hunting Wolf," he snapped angrily. "And he gave me an assurance that none of his men thought of breaking out of the reservation."

"What's that got to do with this, mister?" asked the Kid sardonically.

Van Sillen looked at the Indian-dark Texan, studying the innocent face and the cold red-hazel eyes. He knew that the average cowhand had little but contempt for the United States Army and that here was a man who would have even less respect than most.

"I was just talking to him, back at the reservation,

listening with some sympathy to serious allegations he made against the Agent. Then while I was talking to him, his men were raiding. These Apaches—"

"Aren't Apaches at all," interrupted the Kid. "They're Utes."

There wasn't a sound for a long moment. Overhead a couple of buzzards whirled on wide spread wings, waiting in the hope that a meal would be left for them. On the ground van Sillen looked again at the Kid, noting once more his youthful appearance.

"They are *what?*" he demanded.

"Utes, soldier, *Utes!*" the Kid replied, his eyes on van Sillen. The young captain was handsome, his hair light colored and his moustache small, trimmed neatly. "Young bucks offen some reservation."

"They look like Apaches to me," van Sillen replied.

"That's how they're meant to look."

"Asking your pardon, sir," said the sergeant, his voice a Texas drawl. "The captain can rely on anything the Ysabel Kid says as being right, about Indians."

Van Sillen might be new to the West, he might not know much about soldiering on the frontier, but he had brains and the sense to know when he was being given good advice. He'd heard other army men mention the Ysabel Kid's name in connection with Indian savvy.

"You'd best listen to the Kid, soldier-boy," Comanche put in hotly. "He's fought more different tribes than you've got shiny buttons on that fancy uniform. He didn't come out here after the Injuns were all beat and safe on reservations."

A hot flush of anger came to Amanda Akins' face at the disrespectful words. She threw Comanche a hot and angry look which bounced off the red haired girl's back. A red flush came to van Sillen's cheek, then it was replaced with a smile. In that moment he changed from an eastern desk-warmer to a frontier officer who would get on with the hardy pioneers of the land.

"If you've something to prove these aren't Apaches I would be only too pleased to hear it."

"Why sure, Captain," answered the Kid, giving van Sillen his rank for the first time. "The face marks aren't Apache, they're Utes, or I've never rode attendance to no Utes. Those arrows carry the Ute markings. The war yell's different, I thought it didn't sound right as I come in on them."

"That's what it was," agreed Comanche. "I knew there was something wrong with them, even before I saw those—"

"Those" were the three scalps which lay on the ground. Van Sillen looked down at her then back at the Kid.

"What does that prove?" he asked.

"Apaches don't take scalps. If they take anything it'd be a head or something else which I wouldn't put tongue to before ladies," replied the Kid. "Nope, you can take my solemn word as the biggest liar in Texas that these are Utes."

"That appears to be a rather contradictory statement," remarked van Sillen and turned to his sergeant. "What do you make of this, Sergeant Flint?"

Kane Flint, he'd rode in the Texas Light Cavalry during the Civil War and joined the Union Army straight after it, flashed a glance at Dusty Fog. "Was it to me I'd ask Cap'n Fog there."

Van Sillen turned and looked at the small Texas man. "You are Captain Dusty Fog?" he asked.

"So folks keep telling me," Dusty answered. "Way I see it these bunch are off some reservation and looking for loot. There's only one thing wrong with that. This isn't Ute country and they're not likely to have come this way just on chance."

"You mean the Apaches might have sent for them?"

"That's as likely as a Texas Ranger sending for a Mexican border thief to help him," growled the Kid, "which same isn't likely at all. No Apache'd put on the paint and ride with Utes. And the Lipans have never sided against the whites—yet."

"What does that mean?"

"You ask that Apache Agent, Hillvers," answered the Kid, looking straight at the officer.

"From what I've heard Hunting Wolf's getting tired of being short-rationed and his boys want the war lodge opening. If that happens and the Lipans put on the paint, there won't be a white left alive between here and the Pecos. But the Lipans won't need help to do it and if they did they wouldn't ask Utes for it."

Van Sillen's eyes went to each of the tanned Texas faces and he read in them that the Ysabel Kid was speaking the truth. His eyes went to the men who stood by their horses, his troop.

"Arrange a burial detail to care for the corpses, sergeant."

"I wouldn't want to interfere, Captain," Dusty put in. "But it might be a better idea to take the bodies into town and let some of the old-timers look at them. There's some folks who wouldn't want to believe these are Utes and not Lipans."

That was a sound idea, van Sillen was willing to agree. He would have nothing but the unsupported word of the Texans to go on and his superiors were skeptical about such things. It would be better to have other men look at the bodies and give their opinions.

"See to it, Sergeant," he ordered.

"Yo!" Flint gave the cavalry reply and called three of the men forward. He gave orders for three of the men to drag the bodies to one side. One of the troopers strolled boldly up to the Kid's victim and bent down. He was a brash, fresh faced youngster who clearly had not been long in the army.

"Leave that one," growled the Kid.

"You wanting to have his hair for a trophy?" grinned the soldier.

"I'd leave that to your kind," answered the Kid coldly.

Straightening, the young soldier grinned what he thought was a hard grin. His right hand went to the flap of his holster then he froze solid, for the Kid's old Dragoon Colt was lined on him, the hammer drawn back.

"One thing you'll learn out here, soldier, happen you live long enough—which same ain't likely—is never to start in to touch a gun unless you can get it out a whole lot faster than the other man."

The Kid spun the Colt on his finger and twisted it to slide it back into leather. The young soldier stood still, not knowing what to do. Comanche Blake's eyes glowed with amused contempt as she said:

"And soldier boy, the Kid's not fast with his gun."

Van Sillen growled an order which sent the young soldier, muttering to himself, away from the wagon. The captain studied his horses and picked the gentlest of them. He gave an order for the soldier whose mount it was to use it as a harness horse in the wagon team and escort the Akins to their home, then return to the fort. He told three more men to ride along as escort, sent another rider at a gallop to the fort to fetch out the ambulance for the transporting of the dead Indians.

CHAPTER SIX

On The Reservation

"How'd you like independent command, Captain?" Dusty asked.

"It's different from Washington," van Sillen admitted. "Having a battalion of one's own poses a whole lot of problems."

"Sure, I know what it is," Dusty agreed. "Especially after being in Washington for a spell. We had a troop commander in Troop C of the Texas Light Cavalry during the War, he'd been in Washington before the war and about every day used to start his orders with 'It has come to the notice of the Commanding Officer, Troop C' and so on with whatever it was. Cousin Red stopped it in the end, one day he wrote across the orders, 'It has come to the notice of the troop commander Troop C that too many things are coming to the notice of him so would he please shut his eyes for a spell and let us fight the war.'"

Van Sillen chuckled and then lost his smile for a moment as he thought of the number of times he'd placed the same words on his orders since his arrival. The smile came back once more.

"Point taken, Captain Fog. How did you know?"

Dusty looked at the officer with twinkling eyes. "I've seen a bow-necked Washington man or two in my time. And the name's Dusty."

"They called me Ran at the Point," van Sillen countered. "My troop are nearly all recruits, except for the noncoms."

"After three months they should be better than recruits and they'll all have at least that time in. I know Kane Flint. He can throw a bunch of recruits into shape that could be called full trained in less than three months. Try treating them like soldiers, not like recruits and they'll act like it. Look at the way they and you're dressed. That's all right for the boot-camp back East, but a mite rough on them out here. They've seen how other bunches dress and they resent having to wear full uniform."

"But regulations—" began the officer.

"I think it was General Grant who said regulations were for the strict obedience of fools and the guidance of wise men," Dusty drawled. "That's up to you. I wouldn't want to interfere in another man's interpretation of regulations."

"I always like to hear ole Dusty spout out big words," remarked the Kid. "Even if I don't understand them."

Mark laughed, watching Dusty's face. He was thinking what an officer Dusty had made and would have made under different circumstances. If the fortunes of war had gone the other way, or if Dusty had accepted General Grant's offer after the Appomattox,* the small Texan might have gone far in the Army. Dusty would now hold rank of major at least or more likely be a colonel commanding his own regiment. Yet for all that Mark did not think his small friend would have been any happier than he was as segundo of the O.D. Connected ranch.

Van Sillen rode in silence for a time, listening to the Texans who were now arguing over some incident in their lives. Now it had been pointed out to him he saw where he'd made his mistake with his troop. They'd volunteered to come west with the words of old soldiers ringing in their ears. Tales of relaxed discipline, of a life free from the dull routine of the eastern garrison with its polish and parade. On arrival at Fort Apache they found the routine was still the same with the disadvantage of dirt, dust and heat to complicate it. He decided he would start gradual easing off and allow his men to act like the troopers they'd seen on their way from post to post heading west.

They were now at the foothills and the trail they followed was along the bottom of a valley, the sides rising up on either side bush and rock covered. It was a place where an ambush could easily be laid and would be hard to avoid. Ahead the valley walls closed, the bushes and rocks went up and steep, sheer cliffs were on each side of the trail. Van Sillen pointed ahead, towards the opening.

"The reservation begins at those walls."

Surveying the hard rocky ground and the sheer walls the Kid grunted. "It sure looks like real reservation country. The leavings the white folks don't want."

***

*The offer made in *The Fastest Gun in Texas*.

Van Sillen did not reply to this, for he knew that in most cases the words were true. The usual Indian reservation was area the white man did not want, or if it was not, the Indian would soon find himself being moved to some less useful stretch of land.

"Man, I've never seen range like this except in Texas," breathed Mark.

"It's fair land—for an Indian reservation," agreed van Sillen. He looked at the Kid with a smile playing on his lips. "That's right, this is the Lipan Apache reservation. Almost a hundred and fifty square miles of this basin, with walls like these all around it."

The Kid grinned. He pointed to where a light flashed from one side, up on the wall. Across the range another answered it, sparking twice, then going and leaving nothing.

"By now Hunting Wolf knows we're on our way," he drawled. "Not bad for a bunch of savages. I bet that scout up there has let him know how many of us there are, the color of our hosses, everything."

"Can they do that with signal glasses?" inquired van Sillen.

"The Comanche could, and I reckon the Apaches can. There's not much about war we can teach them, except for cold-blooded murder."

Dusty's eyes were searching the land, looking it over. The walls of the basin, if a basin it was, rose steep and sheer, there did not look to be many places where even a man on foot could climb up and out. If this wall went all the way around, and van Sillen said it did, a man would find it perfection, open range grazing combined with the benefits of fenced pasture. He could run a herd in here and allow it to grow fat with only a quarter of the men necessary to handle such a range.

"There's no other way out but this one?" he asked.

"None that I can make out," answered van Sillen. "There are a few narrow passes a man might use, most of them impassable except on foot, and one a single man on a horse could use."

Dusty and Mark's eyes met, the same thought in both heads. Here could be a reason for a man to try and get the Lipans moved. It would have to be a man in authority, one who could make trouble.

The trail they followed was nothing more than the wheel ruts left by the supply wagon and the herd of cattle which were sent fortnightly to the Lipan village on terms of the treaty. This magnificent range would feed their horses but soon any game in it would be killed off and more would not get in, or not enough to keep an Apache village.

"The trouble with this is you never really know whereabouts the village is going to be," van Sillen explained. "They move regularly to avoid overgrazing the land. They run a good herd of horses down here."

"Come to think of it then, Indians are real smart," drawled the Kid.

"Not so smart," came the officer's smiling reply. "My forefathers were in the party who bought Manhattan Island. I suppose yours came over on the Mayflower?"

"Nope, they were here when the Mayflower arrived," answered the Kid. "And I reckon the biggest damn-fool mistake they made was letting you white folks get in here at all."

The Apache village lay by a stream, a loose group of wickiups.

A bunch of yapping cur dogs came hurling from the wickiups, back hair ridged up and tails half curled between their legs. They came to a halt at a safe distance.

Comanche Blake had ridden in silence so far, watching these Texans, just a little embarrassed at the company of the young army officer and most of the time with her eyes on the Ysabel Kid. She'd done so for a purpose, she was showing him that even a Fox Lodge woman knew her place in the company of her man and his tribal and lodge brothers. She'd ridden slightly behind the others, in the place of a woman.

The girl looked towards where, dignified and stately, Hunting Wolf with the other old-man chiefs and the medicine men and women came forward to greet their distinguished guest.

The Kid stepped forward to face Hunting Wolf. The deep throated Apache rolled from his tongue with hardly a pause. "Greetings chief of the Lipan Apaches. My brothers and I come in peace, our weapons not in our hands. We come to make talk with you around the council fire."

The chief's eyes went to the Kid's young-looking face and his head gave an almost imperceptible nod. Now he saw why this so young-looking ride-plenty could speak Apache. There was Indian blood here, there had to be.

"Our council fire is open to any who come in peace," he answered formally and waved a hand toward the fire where he and the group with him had been standing.

The men squatted around the fire and a stool was brought for van Sillen who had never mastered the difficult art of settling comfortably on his heels. The cowhands, like the Apache, found it easy, for they were more often out of a house than in it and ate a good portion of their meals in this manner.

"I have bad and serious news, Hunting Wolf," van Sillen said. "A wagon has been attacked by Indians."

There was little on the expressionless faces of the

Apaches to show what they made of this statement. For a moment none of them spoke, then Hunting Wolf asked, "Apaches? My people did this?"

For a moment again there was a pause, then the young officer made up his mind and answered:

"No, I believe it was a stray party of Utes. The Kid here says it was. Would the Utes be on the reservation?"

It was brutally put and Comanche Blake glanced at her horse and the Winchester carbine. However, there was no sign of anger from the group of Apaches and Hunting Wolf was still holding his pipe in his hand. He accepted the tobacco pouch van Sillen offered and the girl relaxed. If the chief had refused the gift of tobacco it would have been long gone past the time to get out of here.

"Would you let cur dogs on to your land, Captain?" asked the chief. "You may bring your men to search these lands from end to end but they will find no Utes."

"Your word is enough, Hunting Wolf."

"Are there ways men could get into the reservation without being seen?" asked Dusty Fog.

The chief looked at the small man, seeing beyond just a small, insignificant looking Texas cowhand. "There are few ways that a man could come into our lands. Fewer still where a man could ride in on a horse. We can have guards on every entrance and close this land of ours if need be."

"Chief, I'd admire to see your treaty from the White Father in Washington," Dusty went on.

Hunting Wolf made a sign and one of the party rose to head for the medicine wickiup. He returned with a U.S. Cavalry despatch case which he handed to the chief. Carefully Hunting Wolf opened the case and took out a flat, thick sheet of stout paper. He handed it to Dusty who started to read, then the chief looked at the Kid.

"Who is this one?"

"The Indians in Texas call him Magic Hands," answered the Kid in Apache.*

Dusty read through the treaty, it was as he expected. In return for their services in the campaigns against the Waco, Comanche and Kiowa tribes the Lipan Apaches were given the basin in which they now stood. The Apache Agency would supply the tribe with a laid down amount of food, enough to keep them in comfort. In return the Lipans must keep the peace and never leave their reservation to make war unless they did so to fight for the United States. If the Lipans broke their promise the land would be forfeit. It *was* as Dusty had expected. He handed back the paper and heard the rapid flow of talk between the Kid and Hunting Wolf. The Kid turned his face, a broad grin on it, to Dusty.

"I was just telling Hunting Wolf what the Indians call you. He allows to see you make your magic."

At the moment Dusty could quite willingly have strangled the Kid for he never liked to show off his skill with his matched guns. Yet he knew there was more than just idle boasting behind the words. The Apache were fighting men and nothing gained their admiration more than skill, superlative skill, with any kind of weapon. So Dusty came to his feet and looked around for some suitable target. It was Comanche Blake who found them for him, a couple of small Apache clay pots about the size of beer bottles. She'd heard of a trick Dusty Fog could do and knew that it, more than any other, would be what the chief would want to see.

Tossing one of the pots to the Kid, Comanche walked

*How Dusty gained the name is told in *The Devil Gun*.

away from the fire and halted. The Kid guessed which trick she was hoping to see and moved to her side. Dusty came to his feet and stood facing the other two, his hands with thumbs tucked into his belt. They were about fifteen feet away and separated by some six feet each holding a pot and watching him.

Mark sat back watching, as were all the others. He knew how difficult was the trick Dusty was about to perform. It was one Mark, for all his skill, had never been able to master and only Dusty's ambidextrous prowess, an early defense learned to off-set his lack of inches, enabled him to do it.

Two arms drew back and the two pots sailed up into the air. Dusty Fog's hands crossed and the matched guns were out in a flickering move. He did not appear to take aim, but the guns spat at almost the same instant. Dusty's eyes had tracked the two targets, his mind lining the guns and when they roared he knew just where the bullet and pot should meet. There sounded a flat crash as both pots shattered and the silence could almost be felt as the guns went back to leather and the bits of pottery fell to the ground.

"Magic Hands," repeated Hunting Wolf. "Well is he named."

Shinqua had joined the group in time to see the shooting, his eyes went to Mark's great size and a grin came to his face. "It was well done, ride-plenty," he said in Spanish. "But could any white man move that rock by the stream?"

All eyes went to the huge rock which stood at the edge of the water. The young braves had been trying to lift it earlier in the day, but only he had succeeded in raising it from the ground and over his head.

Mark Counter pushed himself erect and walked forward, towards the rock. He examined it carefully from all sides, guessing at its weight. That was a fair chunk of rock all right and it would test a man's muscles to lift it. Without a word he removed his gunbelt and passed it to Shinqua, then stripped off his shirt.

Stepping forward Mark tested the rock, making sure he could get a good grip on it. Then he bent and started to lift. The watchers held their breath as slowly the heavy rock started to rise from the ground. Mark's muscles rolled, writhed and expanded, sweat poured down his face and soaked his skin but the rock was going up. He changed his grip slightly and heaved, the rock was over his head, held in both powerful hands. For a full five seconds he stood there, then lowered it under control to the ground again.

"That's a tolerable heavy rock," he remarked, resting both hands on top of it.

"We are men together, big one."

Mark laughed, putting on his shirt, then strapping the gunbelt around him once more. The two men faced each other, big men, strong men, proud of their strength. For a moment Shinqua looked at Mark, then held out his hand to be shaken.

"They are two of a kind," Hunting Wolf remarked, his eyes going to the Kid. "And you, *Cabrito*, what of you. Your friend Magic Hands is truly named with his revolvers. The big one is strong with the strength of three men. What can you do?"

The Kid laughed and looked around. On a rock over a fire hung a side of beef. It was twenty yards away and sideways on, not a large target. His right hand went down, the razor edged bowie knife was out, gripped for a throw. The black shirted arm whipped back and the knife flashed out, turning over then sinking deep into the meat.

Hunting Wolf nodded in approval, skill with a knife was something an Apache could understand, for they were knife fighters with few equals.

"How about Nogana?" asked the Kid.

"My men went out and made a search this morning. Whoever did the shooting was careful to hide his tracks. The braves found nothing. Nor could they find any sign to help them where your friend was shot."

Van Sillen had been wondering how to ask the same question and he suddenly saw what the Kid had been doing. They'd been getting the confidence of the chief and the Apaches before asking the delicate question. Asked on arrival it would have been met with evasion and the truth hidden. Now the Apaches knew they were among friends. Van Sillen had learned a valuable lesson this day.

"Could a white man have hidden his tracks that well?" Dusty asked.

"There are some who could, very few though. It was more like Indian work."

"Or a half-breed?"

The chief looked at Dusty Fog and his face was impassive. He neither confirmed nor denied the words. They both knew which half-breed Dusty meant, for the chief had no illusions as to the character of Hillvers' interpreter, No-Nose.

Van Sillen was looking up at the sky, he could tell that it was late afternoon and he wanted to get back to the fort.

"You will come again, Magic Hands?" asked Hunting Wolf, rising to see his guests off. "For you are a man of wisdom and a leader of men. It is right that such a man should come to talk with a chief."

"I'll come again," promised Dusty, then he looked around him at the rolling plains of the reservation. "There is no game left here now, Hunting Wolf?"

"A little, a few deer, but that is all."

"Soon the Lipan will have to find a way of keeping himself. There is grazing for horses here. Good horses such as the cavalry or the ranchers would buy. Think on it, Hunting Wolf. Your people could make money enough to become independent of the agent."

It did Hunting Wolf credit that he saw the wisdom of Dusty's words. The Apache was a warrior, a hunter and cared little for any other kind of work. One thing he did know was how to handle, breed and raise horses. Given some good bloodstock to raise the standard of his horses he might, in this basin, raise fine stock, and for such there was always a market in the West.

"This would take much thought, Magic Hands," Hunting Wolf stated gravely. "It will take much talk around the council fire, for it is a new way of life."

CHAPTER SEVEN

Hillvers Makes an Offer

They reached the valley which led to the open range from the reservation.

"Miss Blake," said van Sillen and the girl looked towards him. "I wondered if you would care to attend a small dinner at the fort. I am afraid you would be un-chaperoned, but I think you'd be safe in the company."

The girl laughed. "Nope, sorry, Captain," she replied. "I've got to make my place before midnight or I'll have old Dingle and Pike hunting for me."

"Then how about you, gentlemen?" the young captain went on, turning to Dusty and the others. "I've a really good cook and would like a chance to discuss things with you."

Dusty thought this over for a moment. Red and Sue would not be expecting them, knowing full well the uncertain habits of the floating outfit. There would be time to head for the S-B the following day and a council of war with the fort commander might be to everyone's advantage.

"I'm on," he finally said. "How about you, Mark?"

"Why sure," agreed Mark.

"Never thought of me as a gentleman," drawled the Kid. "Anyways we can't let this here young lady ride the range unchaperoned. I'll see her to her home."

"That'll be useful," scoffed Comanche. "Then I'll have to show you where the S–B is so you don't get lost."

"Why, sure, I likes riding with a real pretty gal, when there's one around. If there isn't I'll ride with whatever I can get."

Comanche's temper boiled up and poured out in a flow of language which would not have disgraced a mule-skinner. Then she swung her roan from the other horses and with it keeping pace to the Kid's big white, headed across country towards her place.

Dusty and Mark watched the Kid and Comanche riding away, then their eyes met and the same thought was in each head. Over the past year or so they'd seen first the leader of the Wedge trail crew, Stone Hart, then Red Blaze, Johnny Raybold and Rusty Willis succumb to the fatal charms of a woman and sink unresisting into the bonds of matrimony. They'd seen the change which came over their erstwhile, reckless and wild friends, now settled down and becoming family men. Could the Ysabel Kid, wildest, most reckless of them all, become the next to go?

"What do you think about Hillvers, Dusty?" asked van Sillen. "I realize it is a most improper question to ask, but I'm trading on a friendship which has lasted through good and bad for at least four hours."

Dusty grinned. Randolph van Sillen was going to make a real good officer. "A bad one," he opined. "Some slick from the little I saw of him. Tough when the going stands easy, but keeping back and hiring his fighting done when it looks like things will be rough."

"Typical of the worst kind of Indian agent," Mark went on. "There's good ones among 'em. Good as a Texan, nigh on—nobody's as good as a Texan unless its another Texan."

"Do you think he'd short ration the Lipans?"

"He'd short ration his own mother if he thought there was profit in it. You can tell what sort of a man he is by the scum he hires. That sheriff and deputy, they're his men, so are those two hired guns and that breed. A man who has to hire as poor as that can't be any good."

In his short time out West van Sillen had grown used to the way these cowhands could size up a man's character. Dusty and Mark were only giving him more examples of it. He had sized up the agent in slightly more flattering terms himself and wondered if his guess was right.

"Thing I don't get is where the supplies are going," Dusty remarked. "Hillvers wouldn't take a chance on short rationing the Apaches just to let the food go to waste."

"Who supplies the beef for the reservation?" asked Mark, looking at van Sillen, and thinking of one answer to the question Dusty put before them.

"Hillvers. It was one of the reasons he got the post as agent. He owns a fair sized ranch over the county line and has a contract to supply the reservation."

"Then he's getting it coming and going. Short rations

the Apaches," Mark guessed. "And still has the stock to sell on the open market."

Dusty had already thought of that but he was sure the true reason went much deeper. His mind pictured the great basin of the Apache reservation and what it was so easy to become. In that moment Dusty could almost see a reason for Hillvers short rationing the Indians. There was the clause in the peace treaty, placed there to keep the Apaches off the warpath on pain of losing their reservation. A man in the right position could stir the Apaches up, drive them to break the clause and all the magnificent grazing land would be thrown open for sale.

"One thing you want to watch, Ran," he warned, "if you're fixing to go up against Hillvers, is make sure you've got certain proof against him. He'll have a lot of backing to hold down a post like this."

"I believe it was General Hardin of the C.S.A. who said politics are the curse of a career officer," van Sillen answered with a grin.

"Likely," agreed Dusty. "Although I can never member hearing him say it."

The night was falling as the men rode along Geronimo Street on towards the store. There were a few people on the street although the piano was going in the saloon and sounds of laughter came to them. The few people who were out and about paid no attention to the riders.

The sentry at the gate, smart and tidy looking, brought his Springfield carbine up in a small salute as the fort commander passed him. Van Sillen showed the two Texans to the officers' stables, there were two empty stalls and into these the paint and bloodbay were placed, the heavy kak saddles left hanging on the burro. Van Sillen swung his McClellan saddle on to the ridge of the burro; this was a rack shaped like an inverted V and always used by a cowhand if he could, when leaving his saddle. The trooper who had come on the run brought water, grain and hay nets for the three horses, attending to van Sillen's mount but leaving the Texans to enter the stalls with their big stallions.

"You've got some fair stock here, Ran," Mark remarked, as he looked at the good horses in the stalls.

"Yes, I think we might breed some decent horses with their help and the Apache herd."

Sergeant Flint came up, saluting, giving his report. The two lieutenants of the fort were off the post on duty and van Sillen nodded. "Tell my cook I'll want dinner for three in that case."

"Hillvers and Colonel Akins are here, Captain, sir," Flint answered.

"Make it dinner for five then."

"Said Colonel Akins's some riled," Flint warned. "Come in with Hillvers, breathing fire and wanting action."

"I'll go and see him as soon as I've arranged tomorrow's orders of the day," van Sillen stated. "Will you show Captain Fog and Mr. Counter to my quarters and tell my striker to see they have everything to wash and tidy up."

By the time van Sillen finished the orders, leaving his orderly room corporal looking puzzled but pleased by the relaxing of dress orders, he found his guests were washed, shaved and tidied up. He took time to tidy himself up, not wanting to go in for what he knew must be an interview which would not satisfy Amanda Akins' father.

Hillvers, wearing a broadcloth suit, a plain white shirt and a large bow tie of a style which had recently become

the rage back east, was standing by the window and
looking out as the door opened. Colonel Akins was at
the table, pacing the room in the restless way of a big
and important man kept waiting by a relatively unim-
portant captain. He wore an expensive broadcloth suit of
rather out-of-date cut, but his shirt was silk and his tie
set in the height of good taste. All in all Colonel Akins
made a commanding figure and he was well aware of it.

"May I ask, sir," he boomed as van Sillen entered,
"what you have done about this outrage. It's coming to
something if honest and harmless, defenseless women
are to be attacked by marauding savages that have the
protection of the United States cavalry. Have you arrested
those responsible for the attack on my family?"

"Not yet."

"Why not?" Akins bellowed, he did not spare the
Texans a glance although the Indian agent was looking
at them with cold, unfriendly and not entirely unworried
eyes.

"Because I'm not satisfied that the Lipans were responsible for the attack and I haven't found the Utes who
made it," van Sillen explained.

"Utes?" snorted Hillvers. "Utes in this part of the
country?"

"That's right. Utes and in this part of the country,"
replied the captain.

"How would you know they were Utes, van Sillen?"
Akins barked. "You haven't been out here long enough
to—"

"The man who told me has been here long enough to
know," interrupted van Sillen politely. "He knows more
about Indians than most of the people in charge of them."

"That sounds like one at me," Hillvers growled.
"Who's been telling you about Indians—Al Sieber?"

"The Ysabel Kid."

Hillvers mouth shut like the jaws of a bear trap. The Ysabel Kid's name was well enough known in Indian Bureau circles and it was a name that did not give any crooked reservation agent joy. It gave Hillvers even less joy, for he remembered the third Texan who'd come into the town in time to aid Red Blaze. His name had been mentioned, it was the Ysabel Kid.

Akins opened his mouth to say something, for he'd never heard of the Kid. His eyes went to the two Texans again as Dusty moved forward and spoke:

"The Kid doesn't make mistakes, mister."

Akins lost some of his pomp. He held his military title to a commission in the Civil War, it was a commission which gave him rank without the tedium or danger of going near the fighting line. He'd heard that small Texan's tone before. It was that of a tough fighting officer addressing a desk-warmer in time of war.

"Colonel Akins, I don't think you know Captain Fog and Mr. Counter. Dusty, Mark, this is Colonel Akins and I think you know Mr. Hillvers."

The introduction was smoothly made and took the wind out of Akins' sails. He might not have heard of the Ysabel Kid but he *had* heard of Captain Dusty Fog. He saw now how so insignificant a man could command such a tone of voice. He nodded a frigid greeting and Hillvers did not make a move to greet the two Texans.

"These are the two, or two of the men who saved your family," van Sillen went on, to Akins.

Whatever his faults Akins was a man who really loved and cared for his family. He was grateful to the men who'd saved his wife and daughters from the attacking Indians and this was unusual, for he rarely had anything to be grateful over. He sought some way to show his thanks but the words stuck in his throat.

"I don't suppose you would care to come to work for me?" he asked, if they did he could pay them well and they might even bring some order to the chaos in which his ranch appeared to be falling.

Dusty shook his head, smiling. He knew the thoughts behind the offer and knew that given a chance Akins might make a good man out west.

"We're full hired. Ride for my uncle, Ole Devil Hardin. I don't reckon we could see our way clear to change."

"Will you be staying on long in Apache County, Captain Fog?" Hillvers inquired with an ingratiating smile.

"Not long."

The answer was cold, lacking in any cordiality. Hillvers changed his words before they were spoken. It had been on the tip of his tongue to offer Dusty, Mark and their absent friend top wages to work for him. Now he saw there was no chance of their ever working for him. He decided to try another idea.

"I've a herd of about five hundred ready for shipment out at my ranch," he said persuasively. "If you would care to trail boss them to the San Carlos reservation and the Army buyer I would offer you fifty percent of the price. It is on your way back to the Rio Hondo country."

Akins looked at Hillvers with cold eyes, although on the face of it the offer was a very good one. He tried to read some expression on the faces of the two Texans but failed to do so.

"No go, *hombre*," Dusty answered. "We're staying on here to help Cousin Red for a spell."

"Sheriff Gren was worried about having two men with reputations for being fast guns in his county," Hillvers went on. "We don't want shooting here."

"I'll bet you don't," put in Mark.

Van Sillen looked at his guests, he could see the deep flush of anger on Hillvers' face and tried to act as peace maker. He steered the talk to the less dangerous ground of the forthcoming dance, with an inquiry to Akins about the likelihood of Amanda coming in.

The captain's striker, a white haired trooper who'd been a recruit in the days when Colt's first model Dragoon revolver was brought into service, came into the room and announced dinner was ready. Van Sillen felt relieved as he ushered his guests into the dining room. The room was a clear indication of the man who used it and offered more comfort than the usual run of officer's quarters. Van Sillen had money of his own and spent it on his comforts. The room was well and comfortably furnished and without the usual hard and uncomfortable issue furnishings.

The food was good, the wine brought in by the striker of a vintage rarely found on the frontier. The conversation over the meal was light and entertaining.

The table was cleared, the men stood with tobacco burning and the sense of well being which comes from a good meal spiced with good conversation. Hillvers must have thought the two Texans had mellowed, for he faced van Sillen and said:

"I've a complaint, Ran. My foreman told me there was sign that some of my stock have been driven off the range and towards the Apache reservation."

"Maybe the Apaches are hungry," Dusty put in.

"The Lipans are supplied with food from the agency," growled Hillvers.

"I've always considered the issue more than adequate," Akins agreed.

"Why sure, only sometimes the reservation Indians don't always get what they are supposed to have," Mark answered. "Was an agent on the Comanche reservation up in the Indian nations who sold the supplies he was supposed to use to feed his people. Made himself a fair pile of money out of it only if it didn't do him any good. The cavalry found him stood in a hole one morning, what was left of him."

"Had the Comanches murdered him?" asked Akins.

"Waal, no, not in so many words. They'd just dug a hole, put him in it and buried him up to his neck, which hadn't hurt him at all. Trouble was the hole was in an anthill and they poured molasses over his head before they left him. Time cavalry got out there it was too late— the ants had just about eaten his head clean off."

Hillver's face was tense and hard as he looked at the two Texas men. Dusty was nodding his agreement to Mark's story.

"Come to that the agent was lucky. The cavalry troop was commanded by an ex-Confederate officer called Jeb Cortene. I know Jeb. Him and the Kid worked real hard to get those same Comanches to move on to the reservation without spilling a slew of soldier blood. They wouldn't have treated that agent nice had they got to him first."

"Is there a moral to that story?" asked van Sillen.

"Only one, Ran," Dusty answered gently, but he was talking directly to the Agent, not the captain. "Indians are human, they've got feelings. Starve them, lie to them, cheat them and they'll hit back—hard."

"Well, I'm thinking as a rancher, not as the reservation agent," Hillvers growled. "I'm following my right and I've told my cowhands to shoot down any Apache they see on my land looking at my cattle."

"You've done what!" barked van Sillen, his face reddening with anger.

"That's my land, van Sillen. I know my rights. The army can't interfere."

The young captain knew that what Hillvers said was true. Any cattle thief could be shot on sight and there was no court in the West which would convict a man of shooting an Indian, especially one who might possibly be stealing livestock.

"The army can't but I can," said Dusty Fog and the other men all looked at him. No longer was he small, he seemed to have grown until he was the tallest man in the room. He faced the Indian agent, his face hard and cold. His gunbelt was hanging on a peg in the guest room of the building, but he did not need guns to dominate the room. "I'm serving you notice and you can pass it to your men. The first man to gun down an Apache had best be real sure he can prove the Apache was stealing stock. If he can't I'll kill him. Tell that to your crew when you put your bounty on Lipan scalps. And tell them that if Hunting Wolf is pushed on the warpath he won't go alone. Mark, Lon, Red and every man I can raise'll be with them. Right outside your door."

The room fell silent. Akins licked his lips as he looked at Dusty Fog. He had seen that kind of domination before and knew it for what it was. Hillvers' face had lost all color and the lips were drawn back in a snarl of hate and anger. The agent was faced down, he knew it. He was afraid of that small Texas man, afraid of him, not of the guns he had worn that afternoon.

Van Sillen opened his mouth to say something when the doors of the room opened and his striker stepped in.

"Major Al Sieber and a company of Apache Scouts have arrived, asking for permission to spend the night," he announced.

Never had words sounded so good to van Sillen's ears.

Al Sieber was known as one of the top scouts of the army in the West. He and his Apache Scouts, a mixture of whites, Mexicans, half-breeds and pure-bred Apaches, had something of a name for themselves in the fighting of the West. They'd brought the Mogollon Apaches to a reservation and held them there until the governor of Arizona Territory decided the Scouts were too expensive a luxury in time of peace. So the Scouts were disbanded. Three weeks later they were formed again. The Mogollons did not fear the regular army and put on their war paint to leave the reservation on a raid which cost far more to put down than the upkeep of the Scouts who held the peace.

"Tell Major Sieber I'll be honored to accommodate him," he replied. "Ask Sergeant Flint to show the Scouts to Block C. Open the stores and give them whatever they might need."

Al Sieber entered the room after seeing his men were comfortable. Behind him came his second in command. Sieber was a medium sized, broad and hard-looking man. His rank of major was a mere title given to enable him to deal with army officers, for he was a civilian. His black Stetson was in his hand, his face was tanned and bearded. He wore a buckskin shirt tucked into cavalry trousers and had Apache moccasins on his feet. He put the hat and his gunbelt on a chair and came forward, hand extended to van Sillen. The man who followed him was tall, young looking, broad and tanned to an almost Indian darkness, through which a pair of laughing blue eyes looked strangely out of place. His clothes were much the same as Sieber's and his hair was long as a bronco Apache's, but it was light brown hair, for Tom Horn, second in command of the Apache Scouts, was a white man.

"Dusty, Mark!" Sieber greeted, releasing van Sillen's hand and shaking with the two Texans. "Say, what're you pair doing hereabouts?" He looked at the captain. "If they've come to enlist don't take them. Ain't neither of them worth a cuss."

Tom Horn was shaking hands with Dusty and Mark, a grin on his face. "Shucks they wouldn't join the army," he put in.

"Sure wouldn't," agreed Dusty. "You mind Johnny Raybold who used to ride scout for the Wedge? He bought in a partnership with Red Blaze and they're running a brand out here."

"We'd call out there if we'd time," Sieber remarked. "Aint seen Red in a coon's age. Where's the Kid!"

"Hoss buying," answered Mark.

"Hoss buying?"

"Why sure, Al. He met up with Comanche Blake's girl."

The full significance of the words was not lost on either Horn or Sieber but they clearly didn't believe what they heard.

"Not the Kid," growled Tom Horn. "Surely not the Kid!"

"The Kid as ever there was," grinned Mark. "Say, have you met our esteemed Reservation Agent, Mr. Burton Hillvers?"

Once more the significance of the words was not lost. If a Texan called a man mister in that way it meant only one thing—he didn't like the man.

"I'll have food brought in for you, Al," van Sillen remarked. "By the way, we had a brush with some Apaches earlier today. I brought their bodies into the Fort and I wonder if you could look them over for me."

"Injuns?" growled Sieber, looking first at van Sillen,

then at Tom Horn. "You mean Injuns on the warpath around here?"

"Yes. They attacked Colonel Akins' wife and daughters but luckily Captain Fog and his friends were able to reach the ladies before they could be harmed."

Akins moved forwards, his face puffing out slightly. Here was a chance to either prove or disprove the idea that the Indians who attacked his womenfolk were not Apaches. Even he had heard of Al Sieber, Tom Horn and the Apache Scouts. If Akins had eagerness in his attitude there was none of it on the face of the Indian Agent. Hillvers scowled as he watched the other men walking towards the door. He followed them, for to leave now would be to invite suspicion that he did not want.

The bodies of the Indians were laid in a row on the floor of the store building. Van Sillen led the others into the building, his nose wrinkled in distaste at the stench which hung in the air.

Dusty and Mark allowed the others to go past them, they wanted to study the reaction of Hillvers and Akins. The big rancher's face lost some of the color as he looked at the still shapes on the floor. One of the bodies was face down, it was the Kid's victim and so Akins did not see the full horror.

For a moment Tom Horn and Al Sieber stood looking at the bodies. The clothing was right, Apache moccasins and all. Then they went closer with the officer lighting their way with a lantern. Sieber bent and turned the stiff head of one body, to look down at the face marks. Tom Horn was rolling an arrow between the finger and thumb of his right hand.

"You say you tangled with this bunch, Dusty?" Sieber inquired.

"Why sure," agreed Dusty.

"Was the Kid along?"

"Right in there from start to bitter end."

Sieber stood up once more and faced Dusty, who now stood by van Sillen. "What the hell, Dusty. Even if you didn't know the difference the Kid'd tell straight off these aren't Apaches."

"What are they then?" asked Akins.

"Utes, Colonel. Part of a fair bunch that slipped off a reservation. I was sent out on scout with a full troop to try and find them."

"And have you found them?" asked Hillvers.

"Not hide nor hair, mister. We ran into rain back there a piece and it clean washed out any sign of the Utes. We came down this way to see if Hunting Wolf had any young bucks who wanted to become scouts for the army. There's going to be a big campaign against the bad-hat Apaches in Arizona Territory and I was told to try and get as many men as I could."

"Will you be staying long?" Hillvers inquired.

"One—two days at most, unless there's some more sign of the Utes down here."

Dusty watched the Indian Agent's face for a moment and caught a flicker of something which might have been relief on it. Hillvers did not appear to be over keen on having Sieber and the Apache Scouts in his area.

"I'd like the names of any braves who enlist," he said.

"I know my job, mister," answered Sieber.

The men left the hut and Sergeant Flint was waiting by the door with a bunch of troopers in their shirt sleeves, carrying shovels.

Hillvers made an excuse to leave the others and headed from the fort. The rest of the men returned to van Sillen's quarters and settled down around the fire. Sieber and Horn were at the table eating the food brought in by the

old striker, but Akins stood by Dusty, a glass in his hand.
By a casual seeming move Dusty turned the talk to cattle
work and Mark caught the message. When feeling like
it Mark could talk of ranching and the work of a cowhand
in a way which explained things even to a man with as
little knowledge as Akins. Now Mark talked, letting the
knowledge of a lifetime on ranches fall, describing things
which Akins had only too recently been finding out by
bitter experience. Then his talk turned to the round-ups.
Vividly he described how a group of ranches in Texas
would join together in a round-up which would cover
hundreds of square miles, clean out range after range
thoroughly, far more so than an individual could manage.* Akins listened, his eyes on Mark's face, and a
gnawing remembrance of Red Blaze and Johnny
Raybold's suggestion for the same thing in Apache
County.

Akins was a thoughtful man as he went to the room
allocated to him by van Sillen; he was staying the night
rather than make the ride back to his ranch in the dark.
The big man was seeing that his only chance of making
his ranch pay was by showing friendship to the Texans
and accepting such help as they would give. The trouble
was he did not know for sure how to go about getting
that help.

"You've got him worried, Dusty," Mark drawled as
he sat on a bed in another room, jacking off his boots
with the aid of a foot placed against the kelly spur.

"Reckon I meant to," Dusty answered, then looked
up as van Sillen opened the door and entered. "Tucked
your pappy-in-law-to-be in safe?"

"One has to look to the future," replied the captain

---

*One example is given in *The Man from Texas*

with a grin. "I've never seen him sit back and listen to anyone before like he did just now. Why don't you take on for him, just for a few weeks?"

"Cousin Red offered to help and got choked off for it," Dusty answered. "The next time it's Akins who's got to ask. You know, I reckon Amanda Akins'd be thinner than on that sketch."

There was a slight tinge of red came to van Sillen's face. Amanda was dressed in an outfit which to be termed mildly was revealing. It had been done while they were out on a picnic alone.

"So'd I," grinned Mark, for he was just as observant as Dusty.

"Well, she's not."

With that van Sillen turned and left the room. He went to his dining room and removed the sketch, taking it to his bedroom and putting it on the dressing table.

The fort was silent, only the sentries and the sergeant of the guard were awake. Through the night No-Nose rode on a mission which had seen him hauled out of his bed by an angry Indian Agent. In the dining room of a small frame cabin the Ysabel Kid was seated on a hard old couch, his arm around the waist of Comanche Blake's girl.

CHAPTER EIGHT

Dance Night in Apache City

Dusty Fog and Mark Counter rode out to the S-B Ranch
the following morning. They were watched by Burton
Hillvers and his men with something like relief. The
Indian Agent was pleased to see them go for a number
of reasons, not the least that he did not care for the idea
of tangling with them again.

Betty Hardin came from her cabin to greet the arrivals
in traditional western style. "Huh, now my shiftless kin
and his worthless *amigos* are all over us."

Dismounting Dusty walked forward and took his favorite cousin by the shoulders, looking at her. Betty's
eyes were alight with pleasure at the visit and she waited
for his comments.

"You're looking well, Cousin Betty."

"Never felt better," Betty replied. "Come on in and see Johnny."

With the social side of the visit attended to Dusty and Mark turned their horses into the corral and caught fresh mounts from the S-B's small remuda. Red Blaze was waiting for them and they left on a tour of the range.

That was the last leisure day they spent, for there was much to do even with the hard work Red and the regular crew put in. The entire crew of the ranch formed lines and worked the country, trying to make a better estimate of how much stock it held. The results were surprising to Red and his hands, for they had found that the range held even more unbranded stock than they imagined in their earlier work.

The Ysabel Kid and Comanche Blake came to the ranch but that was all the others saw of them, for they rode back to her place later that afternoon with a promise they would get together at the dance. Dusty and Mark found little time to worry about it. The Kid had been their friend, nearer a brother than a friend, since their first meeting in the small Mexican village just after the War.* If he wanted to marry and settle down it was for him to decide. They would miss him but they would be able to adjust themselves to that.

Three days later the doctor, visiting Johnny, brought word that the Apache Scouts, with new recruits from the reservation, had left town. Al Sieber had received an urgent call from north New Mexico about Indian attacks and was headed there to see if his lost bunch of Utes were responsible. The doctor also said the soldiers at the fort were all talking about the way discipline was relaxing and how much better it was to soldier now.

*Told in *The Ysabel Kid*.

They were hard working days but the time passed quickly, Johnny Raybold was on his feet and swearing he would attend the dance even if he did no more than sit with the ladies all night. The dance day brought an air of expectancy to the ranch and all the work was finished early. The two young cowhands, delighted to be working and associating with Red Blaze's illustrious cousin and his friend, were all set to show Apache City what a Texan on a spree could do. Hats were cleaned and shaped to the height of Texas fashion, new shirts and trousers were produced, boots given a most unaccustomed shine. Billy Jack dolefully remarked that it was a whole heap of trouble for a man to go to, but was just as hard at it as the others. The go-to-town horses were groomed and saddles treated to a liberal dose of saddle soap, then rubbed and polished.

"You want me to wear a WHAT!" Red Blaze's bellow rang out from his house. It was the frenzied cry of a man pushed beyond all limits.

Sue Blaze, dressed in the mail-order frock, glared at her husband. On the bed lay the suit in which he was married, pressed and neat, by it a white shirt and tie. It was to this latter Red pointed.

"A tie!" Sue answered, her voice going up a couple of pitches. "A tie! You didn't expect to go to a dance wearing your working clothes, did you?"

"Sure I did. I'm going to town for a night out."

"You're attending a dance, Mr. Blaze. You're a rancher now and I'm going to see you dress and act like one."

Red, wearing nothing but the bottom half of his underwear, eyed Sue for a moment. Then a change came over her, the anger left her face and to his amazement she started to cry. It was the first time Red had ever seen Sue cry and he was shook down to his toes. He took her in his arms, pressing her to him.

"It's not often I want you to do anything," she sniffed.

"Easy, honey," he replied. "What's coming over you."

"I just want you to look like somebody," was the sobbed reply.

Red pushed Sue back to arm's length and looked down at her tear-stained face. "Shucks, honey, I was only fooling. You know I aim to wear this outfit."

Sue's eyes met him. "Red," she whispered. "Red, we're going to have a baby."

Red Blaze's hands dropped from Sue's shoulders, his mouth fell open and for the first time in his life he was completely speechless. He stared at the pretty little blonde girl who was his wife.

"A–a–you mean–I—" Red spluttered out the words. "Honey, you oughtn't be on your feet. Say, just lie down and—"

If anything could have shaken Sue out of her tears it was the sight of Red in this moment of agitation. The tears were dried and she laughed, gripped him by the hands, then kissed him.

"I don't mean right now," she said, gently easing herself from his hands as they closed on her shoulders. "It won't be for a few months yet. And the doctor said I should take plenty of exercise. Now get dressed, pappy."

"Yowee!" whooped Tex as he brought the ranch wagon to the front of the houses and surveyed his two bosses. "Man, don't we look elegant?"

He jumped down and walked forward to survey Red and Johnny who were resplendent in their suits, white shirts and ties. He was walking around them like a stock buyer examining a couple of prize bulls. The other hands were gathering. Dusty and Mark leading their big stallions, ready to head for town. They watched Tex as he went around behind the two prosperous looking ranchers.

"Yes, sir," Tex went on. "I do declare it's a couple of senatooooo, yow!"

The last came as his ear was gripped between a strong finger and thumb and twisted hard. Betty Hardin had come from the house and was dealing in a quick and most effective way with her husband's tormenter. It had been a considerable chore to get Johnny into his suit and tie, and Betty did not intend to have her good work spoiled by anyone. With this in mind she led the yelling Tex to the edge of the porch and applied a dainty, but hard kick in the appropriate place.

"They sure look elegant," drawled Dusty. "Like a couple of real ranch-owning gentlemen."

Red gave his cousin a malevolent scowl. "You hush your mouth, Cousin Dusty, or I'll spread you clear over the lower forty."

"Why sure, Dusty," agreed Mark with a grin. "He surely looks too elegant to rile. Wonder how long it'll take him to come to look like Colonel Akins."

Red's face was a study in emotion. Then he looked at Sue and grinned broadly. "Shucks, us solid, sober and upright citizens have to set an example to you wild cow-hands."

The girls went to the wagon and were helped in by a grinning Dusty and Mark. Johnny followed and launched a kick at Mark, who had doffed his hat and was offering to help him climb aboard.

Then with Betty handling the reins the wagon started forward and the cowhands ran for their horses, going into the saddle and forming a half-circle around their bosses.

The nearer town they got the more people they saw, all headed for the big building. The local ranches were sending their full crews in, for the dance was the first to be held and they wanted to make it a roaring success.

There was considerable coming and going around the building and the Akins party were climbing from their wagon as Betty brought the S-B's two-horse team to a halt near them. A couple more women were coming towards the Akins wagon, where Mrs. Akins, wearing her best dress, was about to climb down. The women talked with Mrs. Akins, with much waving of hands and it was clear that what they said amounted to bad news. Celia Akins turned from the wagon and came hurrying to where Mark was helping Sue from the S-B wagon box.

"We can't have the dance," she said. "Nobody thought to arrange for any food."

Betty and Sue walked across to where the other women were still standing talking and Mrs. Akins made the first move.

"Mrs. Raybold, Mrs. Blaze, we haven't made arrangements for food for the dance."

It was more than a olive branch, it was the full olive tree and all its fruit.

"First off we're Betty and Sue to our friends," Betty replied. "What's the problem of that?"

"But what kind of dance will it be without food?" asked one of the other women, eyeing the S-B ladies' new dresses enviously. Her husband had not been able to afford to buy her a new dress since taking on the ranch.

"Not a very good one," Betty agreed, then looked around. "I can see getting on for twenty women here. If we can't throw up a feed I reckon we'll make a right poor showing."

"You mean cook it ourselves?" gasped Mrs. Akins.

"It won't cook itself and I've tasted some of my husband's cooking," Betty answered, then took command with the ease of one long used to making decisions. She turned to where the men were grouped and watching. "Cousin Red, take some of the boys and see to setting fires in the barbecue pits, Cousin Dusty, you, Mark and a couple of the Lazy D boys head on to the range and bring in a couple of steers. Make sure they're carrying plenty of meat. Comanche, take some of the ladies down to Hacker's and see what you can get, flour, stuff like that."

The women recognized the voice of a leader and the rest were all aware that they would have to get to work if they wanted a real good time at the dance. She grinned at Comanche, cast a look at the way the other girl was dressed and said, "We can't work like this, let's see if Hacker or any of the town ladies can raise some old frocks and aprons."

Betty stopped as she was about to follow the stream of other women, eyeing Dusty and Mark, who were standing by the wagon.

"No steers, no food," she warned.

"Won't be wanting steers now," Dusty answered. "Look up there."

Hunting Wolf, Shinqua and Nogana were riding towards town, accompanied by Captain van Sillen and leading a pack horse which had three deer slung across it as well as half a dozen plump looking wild turkey.

"Hunting Wolf shouldn't have done that," Betty snorted, "The reservation's not got game to spare."

"No Apache'd come to a thing like this without a gift," the Kid answered.

The ranchers were gathering together, as their ranch crews tended to mingle and the ranch foremen formed a group. Hunting Wolf studied the ranch owners, knowing they were the heads of this society as he and Shinqua were heads of theirs.

"I have come as invited," he said.

Johnny Raybold stepped forward, knowing the correct thing to do in such a moment. "You are welcome, chief of the Lipans," he answered.

Shinqua bounded from his horse and took one of the deer, gripping it by the legs. With a sudden heave he had the body in the air and threw it towards Mark. The big Texan laughed and caught the dead weight.

The scene was one of activity now, but it was pur- poseful and controled activity.

The men soon found that, beyond getting the barbecue and other fires going and keeping them going, there was little they could do and drifted into town, making for the saloon.

Hillvers and Gren watched the ranch crews, then looked to where Shinqua and Hunting Wolf were talking with van Sillen.

"Five of your boys are in town, boss," Gren said, glancing again at the Lipans. "If Hunting Wolf and that big buck were to get killed down here the rest would be out of the reservation and painted for war."

"Do you reckon it could be arranged," inquired Hillvers.

"There's going to be some drinking done among them cowhands."

"None of those green kids could handle a gun, drunk or sober," Hillvers growled. "Except the S-B crew and they wouldn't fall for nothing like that."

"I don't mean for them to do it. Get the boys ready to jump the Lipans in the dance sometime."

Hillvers looked hard at Gren. Then he nodded. "Tell

them to watch their chance and to watch that damned Dusty Fog."

Cowhands were at play in Apache City. They raced their horses wildly up and down the streets, trying to equal the equestrian prowess of Tex and young Frank of the S-B. Then with wild yells they headed for the saloon and still in the saddle entered. There was some considerable jostling around.

Dusty was at the bar, collecting drinks for the crowd of ranchers at a table.

The Kid entered the saloon, carrying one of the corn jugs, he joined the men at Dusty's table and with the point of his bowie knife dug out the cork. His eyes went to the circle of faces, every ranch owner was here as well as Dusty and Mark. It was obvious that something more than just a social gathering was taking place.

"I reckon you'll be best one for round-up captain," Akins boomed, looking at Red. "None of us have the knowledge."

There was a rumble of agreement, for the rest of the men had already heard Akins' views on the subject. They knew that they must learn about the cattle business from somebody competent or go under.

"We'll pass the word along the prairie telegraph that round-up hands are needed," Red told the others. "That'll get them here. I reckon we can make a start in about a fortnight."

"Then I propose the business of the meeting is done with and we can get down to the more serious business of having a good time," Akins put in.

"Took, seconded, thirded and carried unanimous," Johnny Raybold whooped, grinning his delight at this new feeling of friendliness which prevailed.

The women had worked well, there were tables with

forms stretching across the open ground before the big dance halls. The barbecue pits were blazing and the roasting deer meat gave out tempting aromas while to one side Nogana and her helpers, two women who previously would have been horrified at the thought of associating with an Apache, were cracking the mud casing of the Apache-baked turkeys.

Mrs. Akins acted as controller of the grounds, ordering the men to take their seats and making sure that all were seated before allowing the meal to be served. All was well, the food looked very good as it was brought to the tables. Then it happened.

A man, a big, burly man in cowhand dress and with a low tied gun, thrust back the form on which he was about to sit and pointed to where the Apaches were taking their seats.

"I ain't sharing food with no damned Apache!" he yelled.

A deep and ominous silence fell over the room. Hunting Wolf stopped half-way down to his seat and by his side Shinqua stood still, not knowing what had been said but sensing it was an insult.

The Ysabel Kid was on his feet, right hand crossing to the hilt of his bowie knife, but Dusty was also up.

"No, Lon," he said gently, then moved from the table. He faced the gun hung man. "Mister, there's a whole big country out there. Nobody's asking you to stay on and eat with anybody."

Akins was also on his feet. "I agree, Captain Fog," he snapped, then to the man. "Who do you work for?"

Four more gunhung men moved, sliding into place around the first. The crowd was growling in annoyance at the insult to their guests.

The man could see this might be tricky and he glanced

towards Hillvers for some sign of instruction. Dusty caught the sign, interpreted it correctly then acted on it.

"Call off your hired gun, Hillvers," he said gently but every man in the room could hear him.

Hillvers could have cursed the gunman for his stupidity in making it so obvious. He managed to sound surprised as he answered, "I don't know what you mean, Captain Fog. I've never seen any of these men before."

Dusty smiled, it was a mocking smile. "Likely you haven't. One thing's for sure. If he doesn't get out of here *pronto* you'll not see him again."

"Either sit down and eat or walk out and keep going," went on the Kid, watching the five men. "Or get a cheap grave in boot hill."

The gunman was looking at Dusty Fog, then his eyes went to Mark Counter and the Ysabel Kid who were also on their feet. The odds were good, five to three and in the general mill there would be a good chance of cutting down one or both of the two Apaches.

"I'm not sitting with any dirty—"

Betty Raybold took a hand at that moment, took it before the guns were out and roaring. She was standing by a table on which was a large tin bowl full of hot water for the cleaning of the dishes when the meal was over. A large dishrag lay by the bowl and Betty scooped it up, plunged it into the water, then threw it across the room. Betty had been something of a tomboy, with a reputation in the Rio Hondo of being a skilled rock thrower. Her old skill of aim had not deserted her. The gunman's words were cut off by a face-full of soaking wet dish-rag which caught him full in the mouth and wound long ends around his head.

The gunman clawed the rags from his face and found himself being surrounded by a hostile looking bunch of very angry women, all of whom held something with which to assail him.

"You want trouble, do you?" asked Betty grimly, holding a rolling pin and eyeing the man coldly.

"Coming here and spoiling our meal," snorted Mrs. Akins, who gripped a skillet by the handle.

"You get out of here," went on the wife of one of the two men who did not get a ranch.

The gunman found himself deserted by his friends, left alone to face the wrath of the women. Slowly he backed until he was clear of the table. Then he turned and walked away.

Looking across the table at the Apache Chief, Dusty grinned. "Sit down, friend, I reckon the ladies have things in hand now."

CHAPTER NINE

The Dance

There was no sign of the discomfited gunman and his friends when the men left the dance hall grounds after eating. They'd been seen on their way by the women, who intended that the first dance given in Apache County would go down well and without trouble. These same women were now gathering around one of the long tables to have their own food.

"If the rest of the dance is as good as this we'll have a night to remember," Mrs. Akins said to Betty Hardin as they took their seats.

Betty laughed. She glanced at the other woman with some curiosity. Mrs. Akins no longer looked severe or tried to show off her Boston-inspired superiority to the uncouth Western womenfolk. The change had come on gradually, through the preparation and serving of the meal, for Mrs. Akins found that in practical matters Betty, Sue or Comanche Blake, while being only slightly older than her daughters, were far ahead of her.

"Why sure," Betty finally said, "It'll be a fair dance. I'm going to have to tie that worthless man of mine's leg up to stop him trying to keep pace with the others."

After the women ate they set to work with the aid of any passing man who Betty Raybold spotted, to clear things up outside the hall. It was dark when they finished and headed for various houses to change or to tidy up ready for the dance.

Betty found there was a table by the door of the hall, behind it stood Gren and Sharpe, their badges shining as they prepared to disarm the cowhands who were coming in. She thought nothing of the move, for there was much for her to do. She held the white cloth strips which would serve as heifer brands and picked out men as they passed the table, handing over their gunbelts and receiving a slip of paper in return. The men, mostly young dudes from the East, were surprised when handed a strip of cloth and told they were ladies for the evening, but none of them objected. Betty got as many men as she thought she was likely to need, then went inside to make sure all the arrangements were in hand.

The ranchers' party came towards the dance hall and Gren looked somewhat worried as he leaned on the table towards Dusty Fog.

"Check your guns here," he ordered, although his tone did not suggest an order.

"I just did," drawled the Ysabel Kid. "I've got it all right."

"Nobody goes in wearing a gun," Gren said, his voice sounding even less certain.

"You've got yours on," Mark put in.

Usually the request from a law officer would have been complied with. Dusty, Mark and the Kid were not proddy troublecausing gunmen, they were cowhands who were looking for a good time. This was one time when they did not aim to hand over their guns. They'd seen the five gunmen still hanging about the town and knew there might be another try at Hunting Wolf. With Dusty wearing his guns the attempt was less likely to come and more certain to be stopped if it did come. So Dusty had given the order that they retained their guns and his two friends aimed to see he was obeyed.

Gren looked towards the ranchers who stood behind the three Texans. He could see no support for his actions in their faces. There was a sawn-off ten gauge shotgun on the table near Gren's hand but he made no attempt to touch it. His eyes went to Burton Hillvers who stood just by the door, looking on.

Hillvers saw his chance to blacken the characters of the three Texans, in the eyes of the influential men of the County, so he stepped forward.

"I can't see any reason why you won't check your guns. The rest of the cowhands have handed theirs over and we don't want any horseplay with guns inside. You won't need weapons in the hall."

"We might, Hillvers," Dusty answered. "Cousin Betty and the ladies don't have any dish-rags and your guns are still in town."

Hillvers eyed Dusty, his face fighting to hold down anger. Colonel Akins stepped forward and halted at the table.

"This's unnecessary, Gren," he boomed. "It's not likely Captain Fog and his friends will start fooling with their guns in the hall. You know that."

The other ranchers gave their agreement in a rumble

of approval. Hillvers scowled, seeing his hold over the Eastern-bred ranchers slipping. Previously they would have come along with him, now they were just as solidly aligned behind the Texans.

"A man doesn't need a gun in there," Hillvers repeated, making a bad mistake.

"Then why've you got one under your arm?" asked Dusty Fog.

Hillvers stared hard at Dusty when he heard the soft drawled words. His face flushed just a little redder and he made an involuntary movement towards where a Webley Bulldog revolver was in a shoulderclip under his left armpit. He had been so sure the gun was completely hidden from sight.

"A gun under my arm?" he asked, trying a bluff.

As a try it missed by a good country mile.

"I'll pull open your coat and make sure nobody stole it away while you wasn't looking," drawled the Kid. "Was you to ask me."

Hillvers looked at the Indian dark face, reading the cold dislike on it. He knew the Ysabel Kid to be no respecter of persons and not the man to be hampered at such a moment. With this thought in mind Hillvers gave an angry grunt, turned on his heel and walked into the hall.

"Your boss don't want our guns checked, *hombre,*" Dusty told Gren. "We're going in now."

There Gren had it, peeled, cooked and served up Texas style. He was left with two choices and there was only one of the two he cared to make.

On a raised platform the band, the saloon's piano, a couple of fiddlers, a guitar and a mouth harp, were getting in tune and Billy Jack, appointed dance set caller by Betty Raybold was getting ready for the first dance. The combination of the band might appear unusual, but it was all the musicians who had shown up and the crowd would not mind as long as the music came good, fast and loud.

The room was well filled and Dusty saw van Sillen with the two Apaches. They were seated by the wall, two young lieutenants with them. Nogana was with Sue, Comanche, Celia Akins and others of the younger women. Dusty saw all this as he crossed the floor towards the Apaches.

Dusty's lack of interest in dancing did not appear to be shared by Mark and the Kid, for they were among the first on the floor in a set. They were both good dancers and showed grace and aplomb.

"Hunting Wolf's people have decided to try your idea, Dusty," van Sillen said as Dusty joined them. "I've been given full authority by the General Officer commanding New Mexico to go ahead and help all I can."

"It'll not be easy, *amigo*," Dusty warned, glancing to where Mark and the Kid were following the yelled out instructions from the band stand. "You're going to have to persuade them to get rid of all those bangtailed scrub stock. They're in-bred worse than a Kentucky hill family. You'll want good stud horses, not that sort of blood."

Hunting Wolf nodded in admiring approval. "Horses are wealth to my people, Captain," he said. "A brave with many horses is a man of standing among my people. They will not easily get rid of any they own."

"I'll use my charm," van Sillen replied, grinning broadly. "Excuse me, gentlemen, I see a lady in distress who needs my attention."

Dusty followed the other man's gaze. Amanda Akins was standing to one side of the room and looking remarkably undistressed. "Use your charm on her, Ran," he suggested.

"I have."

"Yeah," Dusty agreed. "I saw the sketch, remember?"

Van Sillen chuckled and walked away to take the girl into a set and dance with her. Hunting Wolf's eyes went to where his daughter, laughing and happy, was whirling around. Dusty saw Betty watching him and was not surprised when, after the next set, she came towards him.

"Cousin Dusty," Betty said. "It's time you were out there and showing us how it's done."

On the floor Dusty was going through the steps, from the corner of his eye he saw one of the five gunmen moving towards Nogana. He also saw the man was wearing a gun. Betty had become separated from him and so did not see what was happening until it was too late. Mark and the Kid saw trouble coming, or sensed it with the instinct of men who rode often with danger.

The gunman grabbed Nogana, pulling her from among the dance set. The girl did not realize there was more to it than just horseplay until she saw the face of the man coming towards her own. Then she started to struggle, at the wall Shinqua saw what was happening and came to his feet, his hand going to his knife. Fast though he was the big Apache was a good five seconds too late.

Dusty left his set and was across the room before any of the others fully knew that anything was wrong. His right hand gripped the gunman and hurled him back away from the girl.

"Hombre!" Dusty's words came out like the crack of a whip. "The door's right there. You can walk out or get carried out feet first."

The gunman's four backers moved, coming up and forming a half-circle behind him. His lips drew back in a sneer. "What's it to do with you, small man?" he asked. "Or do you want—"

Dusty moved fast, acting before any other man in the room could even think of making a move. His left hand lashed across his body and the bone handled Colt came from leather, swinging up to smash under the man's jaw, rocking his head back, then down once more, pistol whipping the gunman to the floor. The move came so quickly that not one of the five gunmen had the slightest chance to counteract it. The left hand draw also came as a surprise, the men were right handed and tended to ignore the left hand in matters of this kind.

Even as the gunmen saw their pard crash to the floor, it was too late. Mark Counter's right hand dipped and the long barrelled Colt came clear to throw down on them. Gren and Sharpe started forward and the Kid faced them, standing with legs braced apart, right hand hanging with the palm turned out, scant inches from the worn grips of his old Dragoon Colt.

"What's all this?" growled Gren as Dusty turned.

"I'm just doing your job for you," replied Dusty. "This's the second try at Hunting Wolf and I've had my fill of it."

"How's he come to be wearing a gun, him and the rest of this bunch?" asked Mark.

Gren looked at the hostile faces of the crowd and thought fast. "I let you in wearing your guns."

"Let us?" The words came from the Kid in a Comanche mean grunt. "You couldn't stop us."

Akins thrust through the crowd and moved to Dusty's side. His eyes went down to the unconscious gunman, then to the other four men. Dusty did not take his eyes from the men but he knew Akins was on his side. Akins was head of the County Commissioners and he could make or break the county sheriff. Dusty knew this, so did Gren.

"Get them out of here, Gren," barked Akins.

Gren's mouth opened, then closed again. He looked around him, hoping for some sign of moral support from Hillvers. In this he was to be disappointed, for the Indian Agent, not wanting to be around when the trouble came, had made sure he was not on hand.

"All right," growled Gren. "Pick him up and get out."

The four gunmen knew how Gren stood with their boss. Even if they had not, under the guns of Mark Counter and Dusty Fog they would have gone anyway. They lifted their pard and carried him towards the doors.

"The County Commissioners want to see you in the morning," Akins went on.

That was what Gren expected. He would not be wearing the sheriff's badge for much longer. He could see it written on Akin's face and the faces of the other members of the County Commissioners who were standing in the group behind the big rancher. Gren had a well paid position in Apache County, the more so since he could augment his salary by working for Hillvers. He would have trouble getting that much money as a mere hanger-on around the agency. With that thought in mind he let his hand drop to the butt of his Smith and Wesson revolver. Then he met Dusty Fog's eyes and saw the mocking challenge in them. The bone handled Colt whirled, spun and went back into leather. Dusty's hands came clear of his belt.

Gren read the challenge. Read it and moved his hand, then turned, saying nothing more. He wanted now to go to the Indian Agent and talk over what had happened, find out what Hillvers planned to do. One thing was for sure, with what Gren knew this Agent could not just toss him aside and would be forced to help him.

Dusty, Mark and the Kid stood together watching
Gren leave, followed by his deputy. Mark slid his Colt
back into leather and the Kid's hand dropped to his side.
They looked at Dusty, knowing him well and guessing
what was in his mind.

"That's twice," Dusty said gently. "I reckon it's long
gone time when we had some words with Hillvers."

"Thought you'd get round to thinking that way,"
drawled the Kid, unworried by the prospect of facing
Hillvers and his men.

It was a good idea but unfortunately for its successful
completion Betty Raybold knew her Cousin Dusty as
well as did Mark Counter and the Ysabel Kid. She knew
just what was on Dusty's mind and she determined that
the dance was not going to be spoiled by his going out
into what might be a gunfight.

The Indian Agent was in his office, glaring angrily at
the men who stood in a group before him. Dusty's victim
was flopped in a chair, a rough bandage wrapped around
his head. Gren and Sharpe were there also, the big sheriff
scowling and Sharpe watching Hillvers with cold eyes.

"You could let the boys try again when Hunting Wolf's
on his way back to the reservation," Sharpe suggested.

"That'd be real smart," Hillvers bellowed back, then
lowered his voice, for he did not wish to have anyone
hear what was being said in the agency. "I asked van
Sillen what arrangements he had made for the Lipans to
stay on in town. They're not."

"So he's sending them back tonight," Gren put in.
"What's the problem. You've got the four boys who
could handle rifles and the Lipans aren't armed."

"They're not. But the cavalry escort who're going
with them are armed. Van Sillen's no fool and he doesn't

trust me since he got to know that damned Dusty Fog. If I send the boys after Hunting Wolf they'll be tangling with a troop of cavalry."

"I'd as soon tangle with green cavalry kids as that short grown Texas boy again," growled one of the gunmen. "That wouldn't be why Turk quit on you, Hillvers, would it?"

"It could be," replied the Agent. Turk, who had been in the attack on Red Blaze, pulled out the following morning, heading for parts unknown. He went with no word to anyone and went without his pay.

"We've got to do something," Gren put in and his hand went to the sheriff's star. "Akins'll get the County Commissioners to throw me out of office. If they check on my books they'll have more than enough to do it."

Hillvers had also given some thought to this matter. His plans depended on the friendship and cooperation of the local law and in Gren, his own man, he had that. With Gren out of office the Texans would make sure that an honest man, one who would be unafraid to deal with Hillvers, was brought into office. They knew most of the best lawmen, were on friendly terms with most and could easily persuade one to come in as the county sheriff for a time until some local man would take the post. Or one of the Texans might take the post and that would be even more dangerous to Hillvers and his plans.

"We'll have to give them something other than that to think about," the agent finally said. "Where's No-Nose?"

"He went out to your place to see the Utes," Sharpe replied. "They're getting restless, want to be doing some of that killing and looting they was promised."

"They'll get their want, if they can handle it." Hillvers growled. "I'm not so sure they can though. Look at the way No-Nose botched that business with Raybold and that damned Lipan girl."

"At near on three hundred yards, and he had to be that far away to be safe, No-Nose was lucky to even hit her hoss," Sharpe growled. "He was doing what you told him, making sure he did it safe and there was no way he could be trailed. Same with Raybold. No-Nose hadn't used a bow in years."

Sharpe had been the one to introduce No-Nose into Hillvers' organization and wanted to make sure the others knew how little blame there was in the half-breed's failure to kill Nogana and Johnny Raybold.

"It would have triggered off what we want," Hillvers said. "The Lipans would've started fighting and Red Blaze would have been the first to shoot on sight."

"What're we going to do about Akins?" demanded Gren, more concerned with his loss of revenue than the failure of the half-breed to carry out his part of the plan.

"Tomorrow I want you and Sharpe to take those boxes to the Utes. You tell No-Nose to make sure the chief knows that he's to hit at Akins' place at dawn on Monday morning and leave a clear track back to the Lipan reservation. Tell No-Nose to make sure the Utes know I don't want anybody, man, woman or child, left alive."

CHAPTER TEN

Comanche Blake Investigates

The dance was over and the task of loading the cowhand revelers completed by Dusty, Mark and the Kid. Some of the young dudes who rode as cowhands for the local spreads had managed to ride home, the rest were either sleeping it off in the back of the ranch wagons, or somewhere around town. It had been the duty of Dusty and his two friends to get as many hands as possible back to their respective ranch wagons and they'd handled the job with their characteristic thoroughness. Some of the dudes came quietly, a couple of the others were inclined to be belligerent and were treated with speed learned while handling drunks in wild open towns.

The wagons, with such riders as could still manage to stay in their saddles, rolled out of town, separating with some noise, even though it was long past midnight. On the trail which led to the S-B, the Akins and Blake ranches were two wagons and several riders, there was some song, a lot of laughter and much talk until they came to the cross roads where a few days before Dusty and the others heard the shooting which led to their fight with the Utes.

The three parties separated, with promises to meet again real soon. Comanche and the Kid rode side by side across the range, her roan keeping pace with his big white stallion.

"Arabella Akins asked me to go over her place to a quilting party next Saturday," Comanche remarked. "I'll have to get me a new dress for it."

"New dress?" asked the Kid. "Way you squalled when you had to wear that one tonight I never thought to hear you say you wanted a new one."

"I'm a woman—"

"If you're not I've sure wasted some time," answered the Kid.

The girl swung around in her saddle and her teeth showed white against the rich tan of her skin. She did not bring out the words which boiled up in her at the interruption. There was something she'd been wondering about and was almost scared to ask.

"Did you tell Dusty you're staying on here?" she asked.

"Nope."

"No?"

"I didn't have to, gal. We've rode together too many years for me to need to tell him anything."

"What did he say?" asked Comanche, for she knew the ties which held Dusty, Mark and the Kid.

"Just warned me that I'd got to take good care of you or he'd be over here and show me who was the boss. He'd likely do it, too."

The two horses walked on, their riders silent for a

time. The range was still except for the night noises.

"You'll miss them, won't you?" Comanche asked, breaking the silence.

"Sure, reckon I will," agreed the Kid. "If I get time to miss anybody or anything, what with running the spread and raising a tolerable large family."

"You'll be making me blush next," said Comanche, her eyes merry. "Anyways who says you'll be raising a family. I haven't seen you bring any hosses over yet. Fact being, I was only saying to Dingle yesterday that—"

Comanche stopped short, almost biting off her tongue in her efforts to prevent the Kid knowing what she'd said to Dingle. So far there had never been any talk of marriage between the Kid and Comanche, not that she could pin down as real talk, and she did not know how he would take the news that she'd discussed the possibility with her hired hands.

"You mean you've been talking with him about it?" growled the Kid and Comanche was almost sure he was angry. "Trust a woman. Feller stops for a couple of days and right off, him being real handsome, she sees him with both feet hobbled under the table, eating her fixings for the rest of his life. Like I was saying to Dingle, fifteen hosses'd be too much for a flame haired gal with a real mean temper."

Comanche did not catch the full import of the words for a moment. Up until the last sentence she was not sure if he was really angry. Then she knew he was not and she also saw the meaning of his words.

"*Fifteen!* You mean that's all Dingle asked for my bride price?"

"Including ole Blackie here," drawled the Kid, slapping the neck of his big white stallion. "I said yes, never gave it another thought."

With that the Kid's hand shot out around her waist and lifted her on to the white's saddle. The roan had grown used to this happening and kept pace alongside the white.

The girl's lips were hot and crushed against the Kid's mouth. Her eyes closed and she crushed to him. Then he loosened his hold and she sat relaxed and easy in his arms.

The rest of the ride was a haze of pleasure for the girl—and ended in a nightmare of horror.

Comanche, still cradled in the Kid's arms and just about to suggest they stopped for a spell, felt him stiffen. She felt and sensed the sudden change which came over him and looked at his face. There was no smile on it, the lips were drawn tight, the eyes cold and savage. Then she was swung from him into the saddle of her horse, his right hand going back to his old Dragoon gun.

The girl looked ahead. It was a moonlit night and she could see well enough. The scene was almost as she always remembered it, the range just as it always had been. Only the frame cabin her father had built as their home was changed, that and the old sod roofed bunkhouse. They were no longer standing, only charred and smoking fragments of timber remained. The corrals were empty—not quite empty—two still shapes lay by them. Even from this distance and in the moonlight Comanche Blake knew who the two shapes were.

The two horses leapt forward, racing across the range towards the house. The roan was left behind by the big white and through the tears of rage and grief which welled into her eyes Comanche saw the Kid swing from his saddle.

Walking to the side of the building the Kid laid his hand on the timbers, guessing how long since they'd been a blazing mass. About sundown at a guess, or just after. That figured. The Utes would hit just as the sun went down, kill and loot, then burn the buildings in the dark where the glare might be seen, although it was very unlikely. That was how it must have happened, before dark the smoke *would* have been seen.

He heard the girl's horse stop and turned, moving fast. Even as Comanche came down from her saddle he caught her arm and held her. Her face was haggard in the moonlight, her hands clenched.

"Lon!" she gasped. "It's Dingle and Pike."

"I know, gal," he replied, his voice strangely gentle. "Stay here."

Comanche shook her head, eyes blazing with anger and full of barely held down hysteria. "I want to see, I want to know if—"

"They're dead," growled the Kid, shaking her hard and pushing her back to her horse. "Don't go screaming-wild on me, gal. Stay by the horses—do as you're told!"

For a moment Comanche stood firm with her hands clenched and hot anger filling her. Then it died as she suddenly realized why the Kid did not wish her to go and look at the two old men who'd brought her up and stayed by her after her father died. She suddenly realized that without the Kid she was alone, had nobody nor nothing.

"Stay where you are, Fire Bird."

The Comanche language was not one of gentleness but somehow the Kid's deep throated Dog Soldier growl was gentle as he used it on the girl. He knew she would do as he asked, so turned and walked to the corral.

Even by the light of the moon he could see all he needed to. The story was as plain as if printed in foot high letters. Dingle and Pike had been saddling their horses when the attack came. They never had a chance. Dingle lay face down, a bullet between his shoulder blades and several arrows in him. They'd been put there after the old-timer was dead. A man did not live for more than seconds with his back smashed by a heavy caliber Sharps rifle bullet. Pike may have got his gun out. The Kid hoped he had, for the old-timer was a fair hand with his old Spiller and Burr percussion fired handgun. If he had got it out there was a chance he would have taken at least one of them with him before the arrows and the Sharps rifle cut him down. The Spiller and Burr was gone, so was Dingle's Dance Brothers .44 hand cannon. The Kid expected that; the Utes were arms hungry and would take the guns as eagerly as they would the horses of the remuda which had been held in the corral.

Gripping an arrow, the Kid pulled if from flesh, looking at the marks on it. He knew even more certainly now that this was Ute work. The arrow told him that, so did the bloody horror which was the top of each man's head.

The Kid stood for a moment, his eyes on the open range and cold murder in his heart. There would be tracks out on the range, Dingle and Pike had produced several jugs of corn liquor and the Utes would take them as loot. A drunken Indian was a careless Indian. They would not hide their tracks so well with a skinful of corn, and given any amount of good luck by the gods of his grandfather, a quarter-Comanche boy might be able to follow them.

Sanity came to the Kid. There were more Utes in this bunch than he could handle alone and at the S-B ranch house was help.

Bending, the Kid turned Pike's body, leaving it laying face down on the ground. He could do no more now, the shovels and other tools burned with the buildings and he wanted to get Comanche away.

"It was the Utes," he said gently. "Get on your hoss, gal, I'm taking you to the S-B."

Comanche was past arguing or even thinking for herself. She turned and blindly climbed astride the roan once more. The Kid swung afork his white and side by side they rode across the range towards the S-B ranch house. Comanche looked back and tears trickled down her cheeks.

"Dingle and Pike were all the kin I ever had," she said, voice husky with grief. "They were with pappy when he fought off Injuns and stood off the Dobies and Groutens. Now they're gone."

"I know, honey. It was over fast. Reckon they never knew what hit them."

It was small comfort to the girl, although the Indian blood she bore told her the two old-timers would have been far worse off had they fallen alive into the hands of the Utes.

"What're we going to do now, Lon?" she asked.

"Ride back to the S-B and leave you with Betty and Sue. Then I'm headed for the fort to see van Sillen. With him or without him I'm taking after the Utes in the morning and I won't rest until the last of them are put under. Then I'm going after their boss."

The ranch buildings were silent as Comanche and the Kid rode towards them, but at the Kid's knock a sleepy Johnny looked from the bedroom window. Two minutes later the entire house was lit and the rest of the ranch crew wakened.

"I'm going to town—" began the Kid.

"We're going to town," Dusty interrupted. "To the fort, not the Indian Agent."

Dusty knew the Kid, knew that in his present mood he would be likely to shoot Hillvers on sight. There was no proof connecting Hillvers with the Utes, none which

would stand up in court. The only way to nail Hillvers'
hide to the door was to get the proof, and to do that they
would have to get the Utes. They could not do that if
the Kid, their tracker, was in jail on a charge of murder.

Betty and Sue escorted Comanche to the bunkhouse
and left her lying fully dressed on one of the beds. They
closed the door after putting out the lamp and Comanche
turned face down, sobs shaking her frame. Betty stood
outside, her face set in a determined manner.

"It wouldn't have helped if you'd let Dusty see Hillvers
tonight," Sue said gently. "You can't blame yourself for
doing what both of us and Comanche know was the right
thing to do."

Comanche Blake lay on the bed, the room was dark
and still. She was no longer crying but in place was a
deep, cold anger. The longer she lay there the more the
anger grew. She was Comanche Blake's daughter; her
father would never have sat back and allowed this to go
unpunished. Nor should she.

The girl rolled from the bed and paced the room, then
she opened the door and stepped out, guessing how much
time there was before dawn. It would take van Sillen
some time to get his men ready for a patrol, even after
Dusty, Mark and the Kid arrived with word.

The rest of the ranch crew were sleeping, they'd had
a busy day and a long night. So none of them heard
Comanche as she caught the roan, found her saddle and
the Winchester carbine. She went to the bunkhouse and
was fortunate in finding a pencil and paper. In her sprawling, rarely used hand, she wrote a message, telling the
others that she'd gone over to her place. Leaving it on
the bed Comanche went from the room and was soon
riding across the range.

The girl reached the blackened timbers of her home,

scaring off a bunch of coyotes which had been sitting in a circle around the still forms by the corral, waiting for one of their number to take a chance and see if this was a careful trap.

Comanche was no ordinary girl. The life she'd lived, her environment, a woman alone with men, tended to make her self-reliant. She was intelligent, capable of thinking things out for herself. Right now she was thinking and planning what she would do.

It would be noon at the earliest before the soldiers could make her place and begin the hunt for the Utes. In that time anything might happen, rain might come and wash out the tracks. She decided to start after the Utes right now, follow their tracks to the camp and then come back with word of where the Army could go. It would save them time and would allow herself to know she'd done something practical to avenge Dingle and Pike.

She turned the horse and started it along the tracks which showed even in the moonlight. There had been twenty or so braves in the party.

Through the night rode Comanche and as dawn opened up the skies she saw a broad stream ahead. The girl felt a quickening of her senses, that was the boundary line between her place and the Hillvers ranch, it was also the county line. The tracks were headed straight for the water and lying at the other side she could see a stone corn jug, emptied and discarded by the passing Utes.

A more prudent young woman than Comanche Blake would have turned back—but a more prudent woman would never have started this in the first place. Comanche rode on allowing her roan to cross the stream. At the other side she saw that some of the raiders had dismounted, including one who wore boots.

"A breed," she hissed, although it was a term which

rarely came from her lips. "The only part Indian in the country is Hillvers' interpreter."

There was more caution in the way Comanche rode on. She was in enemy country in every sense of the word now. Hillvers was sheltering the Utes, that was for sure. A bunch as drunk as this one appeared to be would not travel far unless they had a camp to go to. They would have settled down near the stream and right now been all asleep, too drunk to care what happened to them.

So the girl rode on, keeping in cover as much as she could, never allowing her horse to make any more noise than was absolutely necessary.

A faint sound brought Comanche's horse to a halt. The girl slipped from the saddle, her carbine in her left hand, the right gripping the nostrils of her roan. She remained where she was, peering through the bushes, and in a few moments saw two men approaching, each leading a packhorse, rope fastened to his saddlehorn. The girl saw who they were, saw and recognized Gren and Sharpe.

The two men were riding at an easy pace towards her. They were dirty, unshaven and looked as if they'd missed sleep. Comanche was less worried by the way the men looked than by the fact that the packhorses carried boxes of a type she recognized. They were the kind of boxes the Army used for shipping rifles and ammunition.

"Don't see what the hell Hillvers wanted us to come out tonight for," Sharpe was saying moodily.

"He didn't want to attract any attention, I reckon," Gren replied. "Come out of town like we done in the dark and folk might think it's somebody going home from the dance. Besides, he wants them Utes to hit Akins place tonight, not tomorrow morning."

The girl's carbine was in her hands, a weapon which

she could use with some skill and accuracy. There was murder in her heart as she watched the two men riding towards her. They had no idea they were being watched and Comanche knew she could probably drop both before they even knew what hit them. It would be just like when the Utes hit her home, only this time it would be Gren and Sharpe who took the lead.

With one hand still holding her rifle she tensed ready to spring into action. Then a thought held her. It would be murder and Comanche could not bring herself to shoot, fortunately. Half a dozen Utes came riding from the opposite direction, headed right for Gren and Sharpe. The two men halted. Gren raising his hand in a greeting, then pointing to the packhorses. He did not appear to be happy about the meeting and showed some relief when the Utes came forward.

Comanche watched the group and followed them at a distance. The noise the horses were making and the talk of the Utes prevented them hearing the girl as she followed. Then they passed over a rim and headed down the other side. The girl could hear enough noise to know the Ute camp was behind the rim, in a valley, even without the smoke which was rising from cooking fires.

Flattening down under a bush, Comanche Blake looked towards the camp. She saw all she wanted to see, a large camp, at least a hundred braves. By now the other party had arrived and the braves were crowding around, reaching eagerly for the boxes in which lay rifles and ammunition.

Comanche studied the camp, looking it over and knowing that the army would be hard put to take so large a bunch once they were armed, more so if van Sillen did not know about the weapons. Her eyes were on the women who did the menial tasks around the camp. The Utes aimed to stay on here for a time it appeared, either that or they traveled in more style on the warpath than did a Comanche who would never take his women along.

Comanche moved back from the rim. She worked her way through the bushes, backing quietly, watching the rim.

A slight sound brought Comanche swinging round, she was only just in time. A Ute girl as big and heavier than Comanche was coming at her, a knife held in her hand. The Indian girl was hurling forward.

There was no chance of shooting, Comanche knew it. There was only the chance of her avoiding the slash of the knife. It was lucky that the Ute girl did not know anything of knife fighting. Comanche brought the butt of her rifle around and felt the blade of the knife splinter against it. Comanche did not hesitate, she released the carbine and then the Ute hit her and they reeled backwards with hands driving into hair.

It took Comanche just a brief five seconds to know she had to show the Ute girl how a tough Comanche fought. She knew how to take care of herself and knew hair yanking could never be as effective as a well applied fist. The Ute was driving to force her down and Comanche released the hair. Her fist clenched and sank into the Ute girl's middle, bringing a gasping croak, the hands let loose of her hair and the girl staggered away. Comanche was diving in when she heard a rush of feet and a second Ute woman was hurling at her. This girl was even bigger, with hard muscles a man might have envied. The weight of the newcomer sent Comanche reeling backwards and down. The hard ground almost jarred the wind from the girl and they went rolling over in a struggling tangle of arms and legs. Comanche saw the other girl was getting to her feet holding her stomach and whimpering in pain. The Ute girl had apparently taken all she aimed to from Comanche, for she turned and started for the top of the slope, meaning to give warning.

The bigger Ute girl was on top of Comanche, hands lacing into her scalp and sending waves of pain through her. The girl lifted Comanche's head and banged it on to the ground. Comanche's hands were under the Ute's jaw, forcing her head back, then she lost her grip. Her scrabbling fingers closed on a rock and Comanche brought it round, then drove it up to smash into the other girl's jaw. Again Comanche's head was smashed on to the ground and again she swung the rock. The bigger Ute was hurt, she screamed in pain. Comanche's back arched, then with a heave she threw the dazed Ute girl from her.

Comanche came up fast, shaking her head as she went after the other Ute. The girl saw her coming and screamed out the start of a warning. Comanche dived the last few feet, her arms latched around the Ute's legs and brought her crashing to the ground. The other one was on her feet by now, charging forward and Comanche knew this was the dangerous one. She slammed a backhanded blow to the face of the girl she'd brought down, then dived forward, leaving her to tackle the other.

They fought like two wildcats and the smaller Ute was dragging herself, whimpering towards the ridge. Over and over Comanche and the big Ute girl rolled in a savage hair tearing, kicking, wild swinging fight where everything and anything went. Then Comanche saw her chance. She brought her forehead forward, felt the Ute's nose crush under the impact, heard the scream of pain and felt the hands loosen. Comanche started to tear herself free, her shirt waist stayed in the hands of the Ute and the man's undershirt she wore beneath it was torn open.

The other Ute woman saw Comanche tearing free and

dragged herself to her feet, screaming in terror. She was running and would soon be in view of the camp. Comanche knew she must stop the Ute girl any way she could. Her hair was in an untidy tangle before her eyes, she thrust it back, saw her carbine and felt the Ute she was fighting crawling at her waistband. Comanche kicked, driving the toe of her high heeled riding boot full into the Ute's stomach. She heard the girl's scream, felt the hands go from her, then she dived forward, snatching up the carbine as she landed and firing. The Ute girl who had run was almost at the head of the slope, her mouth opening to scream a warning about the white girl. The carbine centered and spat in Comanche's hands, throwing lead. The Ute girl's back arched, her hands threw out and she reeled forward to crash down the slope in full view of the camp.

Comanche saw the girl going down and knew that she must get away from the woods or she never would. She was levering another bullet into her carbine when she saw the second Ute woman coming at her. The Ute had been hurt, badly hurt by the kick, but she was coming in for the attack again. Comanche felt scared of another woman for the first time in her life. She knew the Indian girl was stronger than herself and that she would have strength to hold on until the Ute braves arrived.

Quickly Comanche leapt in, swinging the carbine around. The steel shod butt crashed into the Ute girl's jaw, snapping her head over. The girl pitched to one side and landed hard on the ground. Comanche did not wait. She was staggering on her feet, gasping for breath, her emotions churned up as a result of the fight, but her willpower kept control and sent her staggering through the woods towards where her horse waited.

Behind her as she staggered through the trees

Comanche heard the yells of the Ute braves, knowing they'd topped the slope and were looking for her. The roan horse was before her, reins trailing. Her foot found the stirrup iron and she dragged herself into the saddle. The world seemed to whirl around her but she clung on to the saddle with both hands and kicked the horse into a run.

How Comanche kept in the saddle she could not tell. Whatever it was she was still sitting on it when the roan waded into the stream which bordered her ranch.

Slipping from the saddle Comanche kept a hold of the reins and booted the carbine to which she'd clung all the time. She scooped water on to her face where the nails of the Ute girl had left scratches. Then Comanche looked back, she saw three riders coming over a distant slope.

Comanche swung into the roan's saddle and sent it forward, making the best speed it could across the range. She knew that she must make her ranch house and fort up, for the three riders were Gren, Sharpe and the half-breed called No-Nose.

CHAPTER ELEVEN

The Kid Loses a Dream

Gren never felt comfortable or safe when among the Utes. He always got the impression they'd be just as happy to take his hair and sink arrows into his hide as they would to kill the dudes they'd been brought in to handle. So he was relieved when No-Nose, eyes dull and showing signs of being on something of a whisky jag, made his appearance.

"Get these rifles out and among your kin," Gren growled, "I want to get back to town as fast as I can."

The issue of the arms was made quickly, going on the principle of first come first served, for there were not enough to go around. Gren was feeling pleased with himself now and the grin he threw at Sharpe was matched by the lean gunman's relieved expression.

Then they heard the sound of screams and of a struggle. They looked up at the rim as did the Utes but the latter showed no more than a casual interest, for fights between the women were not exactly rare.

"Sounds like a good whirl," Sharpe remarked. "Let's have them down here and watch it."

"Leave it lie," No-Nose warned. "The Utes don't take to white men touching their womenfolk."

So the men got on with their own business.

Then a Ute girl staggered into view. She opened her mouth to scream something to the men who were looking up towards her. The men heard the flat crack of a shot and the girl arched her back, then came pitching forward, rolling lifeless down the slope.

Instantly every brave was on his feet and alert, hefting his weapon. The women might often fight, but never with firearms.

"Quick!" Gren roared. "Get up there!"

The Utes did not understand his words, but they bounded up the slope with the three white men after them. For all his bulk Gren was one of the first to reach the top of the slope and he peered over with some caution. There was no sound in the bushes and so he went over the rim top, his Smith and Wesson Russian revolver gripped in his hand. The other men, ignoring the dead girl on the slope, fanned out and went into the bushes fast.

It was Sharpe who found the second Ute girl. He gave a yell which brought the others to him. No-Nose grabbed the shirt which Comanche had lost in the fight and held it out while the Utes crowded around.

"A white gal's," he snarled. "Comanche Blake's I'd say. Look at that gal. She looks like she tangled with a wildcat and you know how Comanche Blake can fight."

Gren glanced at the scratched, bloody face of the Ute

girl as she lay without a movement. He'd seen one result of Comanche Blake's fighting prowess and recognized her kind of work. A second thought hit him, a thought which put action into his limbs.

"Then she saw us," he growled. "We've got to make sure she don't talk."

That was for certain. Nothing and nobody was hated more and dealt with quicker than a white man who armed bad Indians.

"I'll get the Utes after her," No-Nose suggested, looking for a half-breed cousin of his who was with the Utes, having elected to live on the Indian side of the family tree.

"Nope. We don't want them traipsing the country," Gren replied. "Make sure they know to hit at the Akins place tonight, not the S-B. Then get our hosses and we'll take out after her."

Gren and the other two rode their horses in a direct line for Comanche Blake's house, knowing that was the most likely place to find the girl, or some sign of her. From the look of the Ute girl and the length of the fight Comanche would not be in any shape to make good time.

It was No-Nose who saw the girl first. He bent forward and reached for the Sharps rifle in his saddleboot. Then the other two saw the girl as she stood knee deep in the water of the boundary stream, still a good distance away. Even as No-Nose began to draw the rifle he saw he was too late. The girl had turned, seen them and was now swinging back afork her roan horse and heading it across the water.

"Get after her!" Gren yelled. "You'll not hit her at this range."

Comanche Blake rode with death at her heels, urging every bit of speed out of her little roan.

The range was flashing by. The roan ran well, ran with the heart and spirit only a good horse can show. Comanche knew her little roan would run until it dropped. She also knew the dropping was not long away. She herself was in little better shape, that brief pause by the stream being the only thing which revived her and allowed her to stick in the saddle.

Behind her the men were closing the gap, for their horses were fresher. At any minute she expected to feel shots slapping the air by her but did not try to turn and fire although she drew the carbine once more. The ranch was ahead now.

That was when Comanche's luck ran out. The roan staggered and started to buckle forward. She felt it going and kicked her feet free. She lit down rolling, came to her knees and saw Gren was near, had brought his horse to a halt and was lining the Smith and Wesson. The gun roared once. Through the smoke Gren saw Comanche rock backwards under the impact of the .44 bullet. Then Sharpe fired and the girl spun around to go down.

"Got her!" Gren roared.

The carbine was still in Comanche's hand as pain welled through her but she forced herself over and fired. Gren's shot, fast taken, had been lucky to hit. His luck held. The girl's bullet ripped up, missing his face by scant inches and sent his hat spinning from his head.

"Look!" Sharpe pointed.

The other two looked and felt cold fear welling over them. Men were riding towards the house, still distant, but the sun reflected on brass, showing a large bunch of soldiers were approaching. Even as the men looked the party started down a slope out of sight.

No-Nose had eyes far keener than the other two. What he'd seen of that approaching party filled him with fear.

At the head of the party rode four men, three of whom were not soldiers. They were Texas cowhands, one riding a paint, one a bloodbay and the third a huge white. No-Nose did not need any help to know who the men were and he knew how Comanche Blake stood with the Ysabel Kid.

"Let's get out of here," Gren snarled.

"Where'll we go?" replied Sharpe, looking to where the girl now lay face down and without movement.

That posed a difficult problem to Gren. They were cut off from Apache City by the approaching riders. To head back to Hillvers' land would lead the pursuing men to the Utes, for on the Hillvers' range was too much Indian sign to be missed. There was only one way left open.

"Head for the foothills," he yelled. "She's cashed and there's no way they can prove who done it."

The three men turned their blown horses and started away as fast as they could. Gren was thinking fast, thinking with the desperation of the doomed on him. They must make a big circle and come to Apache City where Hillvers would be forced to give them enough money to escape.

Dusty Fog, Mark Counter and the Ysabel Kid rode with Captain van Sillen at the head of half of his troops. Red Blaze followed, riding by the side of the young second lieutenant. Behind them came the troop and in the rear Betty Raybold drove the S-B wagon with Sue Blaze at her side. They were going to help Comanche salvage what she could from the wreck of her home. The soldiers were in their shirt sleeves and wore their campaign hats, they were armed for war and determined to end once and for all the terror of the raiding Utes.

It was the Kid who saw the house and beyond it the

horse and girl. His face lost every bit of color and he
sent his horse hurling forward at a run which left his
friends well behind.

Red Blaze saw what was happening, reined his horse
and sent it back along the line to where Betty held the
wagon behind the soldiers.

"Oh, no!" Betty gasped as Red told her what he'd
seen.

The girl needed no further words. She set her whip
to the team and the wagon went bouncing and lurching
along by the soldiers, after Red who was racing his big
claybank towards the ruins of the house. By Betty's side
Sue clung on grimly, her face set and pale.

The Kid left his horse at a dead run, landing on his
feet and dropping to his knees by Comanche's side. It
needed only one quick look to tell him he'd lost a dream.
One of the bullets had come straight through and there
was a large hole from which blood poured.

Gently the Kid turned Comanche over. Her eyes flickered open, eyes already misting with death. Behind the
Kid, standing rigid as if carved from stone, Dusty and
Mark looked down. Their faces fought to conceal the
thoughts which raced through their heads but their hands
were clenched until the knuckles showed white.

"Cabrito!" Comanche gasped.

"Who did this, Fire Bird?" asked the Kid in the language of his grandfather.

The girl looked up at the Kid, her hand lifted and
touched his cheek, rubbing it gently with the fingertips.
She gasped, "The Utes—Akins' place tonight—going
to hit—it. Gren followed—"

The Kid was hardly hearing the words. He held the
girl in his arms, trying to stem off the death which even
now was welling over her. No doctor could save her.

Nothing could be done except pray the end would be quick and without pain.

"Fif-fifteen horses—one of—them Blackie—Lon—I'm—Lon—!"

The hand fell from the Kid's cheek, falling limp in a way he knew. He knew, although he tried to fight against the knowledge that Comanche Blake was dead.

The S-B wagon had stopped and Betty half jumped half fell from the seat. She'd heard everything and watched Mark bringing back the Stetson which lay beyond the girl's body. The face Betty turned towards Dusty was one he'd never seen before. For the first time in her life she'd lost her self-control and was on the verge of hysteria.

"It's my fault," she gasped, recognizing the hat. "I stopped you going after Hillvers last night—now this has happened because of it."

Dusty caught Betty by the arms, shaking her hard. "Cut that, Betty," he snapped. "You know what you did was right. Now stop it and get a grip of your saddle. If Lon needs help not even Mark or I'm going to be able to give it him. I'm relying on you."

It took Betty a hard struggle to regain her control. Then she turned and found Sue by her. Saw Sue and the look on the blonde girl's face. Her arm slipped around Sue's shoulder and her voice was gentle, but it was the voice of Betty Raybold, not a hysterical woman.

"Go back to the wagon, Sue. This's no place for you in your condition."

Sue tried to rebel. Tried to pretend carrying her husband's first child was not important to her, but she knew she was wrong. At any normal time she would have been as practical as Betty. Right now her place was in the wagon and out of the way.

Red Blaze and van Sillen were by Betty now. The
soldiers were halted some distance to the rear. Van Sillen
looked to where the Kid still knelt cradling the dead girl
in his arms.

"Can we do anything?" he asked.

Betty shook her head. "Nothing. Don't touch or speak
to Lon right now. Just pray for the men who did this.
May God have mercy on them, for Lon will show them
none."

Dusty took the hat from Mark, examining it. Then he
turned and walked back to the others.

"Comanche said something about the Utes and Akins'
place tonight. I think she followed Gren to the Ute camp
and heard something, or saw it."

"What're you going to do?" asked Betty.

"Go after them right now. Hold them down for Lon.
This is one time the law and its due processes can go to
hell for all of me."

Red stepped forward, but Dusty shook his head. "I'm
riding with you, Cousin Dusty," Red said grimly.

"No, go, Red," Dusty answered, knowing that Gren,
Sharpe and the half-breed would not live until the Kid
arrived if the hot-tempered Red rode with him. "I want
you with Ran and his boys when the Utes hit Akins
tonight."

Van Sillen gave his unspoken agreement to this. He'd
not fought Indians and would likely need some help. Red
did not see it that way.

"I aim to go al—"

Dusty faced his cousin and in that moment Red was
carried back to the days in the Texas Light Cavalry when
he'd objected to Dusty's wishes.

Red watched Dusty and Mark swing astride their horses
and turn to ride away, Mark bending forward to look at

the ground as he read the sign of the men who killed Comanche Blake.

For a long ten minutes the Kid did not move. He was cradling the girl in his arms, fighting down the grief which filled him. Then he lowered the dead girl to the ground and stood up. On his face was a look that Betty Raybold had never seen before, a glare of hate in his eyes which was frightening even to one who had known him for many years.

Words rumbled deep and menacing from the Kid's throat. At first Betty could not understand them. Then rememberance came. Some time before her marriage, a noted Eastern authority on Indians had visited the OD Connected. During a discussion on the ways of the Co- manche, he had asked to hear the Dog Soldiers' revenge oath and the Kid obliged by repeating it. At that time, in the comfortable main room of the ranch house, the speech had been no more than a string of half-under- standable Comanche words.* Listening to it spoken with true intent and the full passion of grief, the girl could barely restrain a shudder. Slowly, savagely, the Kid spoke the revenge oath; promising never to give up the hunt until all Comanche Blake's killers were dead.

"Earth, father, you hear me say it!" the Kid finished. "Sun, mother, you hear me say it. Do not let me live another season if I fail."

Then his eyes went to the watching group and for a long moment there was no recognition in them. Then he relaxed slightly and his eyes lost the hate, only the grief remaining.

"Take care of her, Betty," was all he said.

Turning, the Kid walked forward, taking up

---

*Told in *Sidewinder*.

Comanche's carbine and going to his horse. The huge white stallion stood still as a statue, as if sensing that all was wrong in its master's world. The Kid bounded into the saddle. His eyes dropped to the still shape on the ground and with an almost animal snarl of pent-up rage he turned the horse to ride after his friends without a backwards glance.

Tears welled into Betty's eyes and through them she heard the sound of Red's cursing.

Red lifted Comanche's body and carried it to the rear of the S-B wagon, then reverently covered it with a tarp. Van Sillen's men were detailed to dig graves for the two old cowhands and went to work fast.

"I'll likely be with Ran all night, Cousin Betty," Red said as he stood by the wagon, his arm around Sue's shoulders. "Take care of Sue."

"There's only the one way she can get hurt," Betty promised grimly. "And that is after we're all dead."

Gren, Sharpe and No-Nose allowed their horses to walk at an easy pace. This was through no desire to show kindness to the animals, but as a matter of sheer necessity. Those three horses were all which stood between the men and certain death, so although they would much have preferred to be galloping, putting miles between themselves and the Blake place, they could not risk it. If the horses went down as had Comanche Blake's they would be left afoot and at the mercy of the men who would be hunting them. Not that the Ysabel Kid would show any mercy.

"They'll have found her now," Sharpe said for the tenth time. "Likely be on our track."

"She was dead when they reached her. She had to be," replied Gren, trying to convince himself as well as his companions. "We both hit her—"

"We don't know that!" yelled Sharpe. "I only saw her hit once. When you fired."

Gren looked at Sharpe, seeing the raw fear on his face.

"We both hit her," warned Gren savagely. "You don't think the Kid'll bother who did or didn't shoot, do you?"

No-Nose turned, looking back the way they'd come. His hand shook as he pointed.

"Cabrito!" he croaked. "The Ysabel Kid."

"Off the trail and into the hills!" Gren yelled back.

The men had barely swung their horses from the trail when they saw a man riding parallel to them at a distance of about a hundred yards. A man on a big paint stallion and with the butt of a Winchester Model 1873 carbine resting on his knees, the barrel pointing to the sky. One man blocked their way to the hills. One lone man. But that man was Dusty Fog.

"Back! Cut across the range!" Gren screamed.

The heads of the tired horses were turned in a way which would carry them in the direction of the open range. Then Sharpe gave a yell and pointed ahead. Riding on a line parallel to the trail, at about a hundred yards and cutting them off from the open range, was a man. A handsome blond giant of a man riding a huge bloodbay stallion, a Winchester Model 1873 rifle looking small in his big right hand. One man again blocked their way of escape. Just one man. But that man was Mark Counter.

A rush at either man might possibly bring success, for the odds were three to one, but none of that scared trio meant to try it.

One thing was clear to the men. Dusty Fog and Mark Counter did not mean to make a move until the Kid caught up with them. Not unless they were forced to do so. Gren saw this and sweat poured down his face as he realized what it meant. The Kid was being allowed to finish them off in his own good time.

Like trail hands moving a herd Dusty and Mark kept their positions on the flanks. The three men were still not running but were holding their horses for a later dash to safety. The trail rolled on and the distant rider on the big white stallion was in plain sight now. Then Gren saw where they were heading. The opening which led into the reservation was ahead of them.

"Get by there!" he yelled.

It was already too late. Mark Counter's bloodbay had hurled forward and he sat it well clear of the opening, but he now held his rifle ready to shoot. Behind and to one side Dusty Fog was also ready to shoot and cut off their escape. Gren's mouth opened, wanting to yell orders, then he chanced to look back. To his fear crazed mind the Kid was almost on them, although the big white horse and its rider was still a good way behind. With a yell Gren set the spurs to his horse and sent it racing through the opening closely followed by the others. They felt some slight relief as they saw the open land ahead, plenty of good cover for them to hide in. Gren led the way while high over them a signal light flashed, warning Hunting Wolf that strangers were on the reservation.

"I'll make the village, Dusty," Mark said, riding towards his friend. "You stay on here and keep them bottled in."

Dusty nodded, that had been his plan, for he remembered what Hunting Wolf said about sealing the reservation so no man could get in or out.

Mark started his big horse across the reservation, riding with all his skill. He was always a light rider, despite his giant size and the bloodbay was up to carrying his weight when aided by his skill. For all that it was well lathered when he rode into the Lipan village.

Shinqua and Hunting Wolf came from the council lodge. There was a rare smile on the big lodge chief's face as he raised one hand in greeting.

"Greetings, Tall One," he boomed, "You have ridden fast. Do you come to wrestle, or to lift little rocks?"

"Neither," replied Mark, also speaking Spanish and the look on his face drove the smile from Shinqua. "There is trouble. I need your help."

"You ask and it is yours for the taking."

Mark swung from his horse and a sign from Shinqua sent a boy running forward to take its reins, leading it until it was cooled down. Mark told why he'd come as the boy walked away and the two Apaches listened with faces impassive though there was anger in their eyes.

"So the dogs come on to our land," growled Shinqua. "The Hawk Lodge rides. Soon there will be a great killing and three men will scream many times before they die."

"That is not the way," barked Mark and the two giants faced each other. "The men killed *Cabrito's* woman. He has taken the lodge oath of a Comanche Dog Soldier and it is on him that revenge must fall."

Mark did not know for sure if the Kid had taken the lodge oath but was willing to bet he had done so.

"His oath will be honored," replied Shinqua. "Tell us what our Comanche brother wants and we will do it."

"Close the reservation," Mark said quickly. "Make sure that not even a rattlesnake could get out by day or night. Let keen-eye scouts range the land and word of where the three men are be brought to the Kid."

Shinqua gave a wild yell which brought men from where they'd been standing or resting in their wickiups.

His orders boomed out and soon every available warrior was riding across the reservation to reinforce the guards at the exits, following a well arranged plan for just such an emergency.

"It is done, my brother," Shinqua growled. "I will ride with you and take horses for your friends. Three men have come to our land. On our land let them die."

CHAPTER TWELVE

An Account is Paid

Red Blaze was a worried man as the sun went down on the fate-filled day that Comanche Blake died. He stood out there alone, on the porch of the peaceful looking Akins' ranch house, not looking up at the rim where his every instinct warned him the Utes were even now forming, watching and preparing to come down in a rush which would swamp the supposedly unsuspecting house. He stood out there alone, for he thought the Utes might become suspicious if they saw none of the crew around, taken with the fact that the horses had been driven from the corrals and away from the ranch. So Red elected to be the one outside, it was a position of danger.

In the house beyond him and in the bunkhouse and out-building crouched Akins and his men, their guns ready. And to one side, well clear of the ranch, hidden in a fold of the ground, van Sillen and his men waited, ready to spring the trap on the Utes. Everything possible had been done to ensure the attack failed.

The wild yell of the Ute leader brought Red's attention to the rim. His hands twisted palm out and lifted his long barrelled Colts from the holsters ready for use. The slope above the house was aswarm with Utes, charging down in a large bunch and screaming their yells as they came. It was a neat attack and would have taken the Lazy D house by surprise without Comanche's warning.

"Yeeah!"

Red's eyes gauged the distance to the Utes and at the right moment he gave the wild war yell of the Texas Light Cavalry. His right hand Colt, thumb cocked and ready, came up, lined and fired, tumbling the leading Ute from his horse. The Indian went down and Pike's old Spiller and Burr revolver fell from a dead hand into the dust under the hooves of the horses.

At the shot the Akins crew fired a volley which ripped into the close packed ranks of the Utes sending down men and horses. It was well done, without fear or panic, Red was pleased to see. His left hand Colt bellowed and a second brave pitched from his racing war pony. Then bullets were coming at Red, coming from more guns than the Utes should have owned. The porch was no longer a safe spot, for while the Utes were not skilled with their weapons they were firing in enough lead to give some of it a chance to connect.

Flinging himself from the porch Red darted forward to the side of the well and from its shelter cut down another screaming warrior. Lead slapped around him and he was still in danger.

Akins saw Red's danger and with a roar of, "Out and at 'em!" tore open the door of his house to leap forth with a Winchester in his hand. His men followed, throwing lead with speed if not with skill.

Only one thing saved Akins and his crew. The Utes were bunched, more for mutual cover than any other reason, and offered a large target into which even an unskilled shot might fire with some hope of success.

That was the moment van Sillen brought his men into the attack. They came sweeping out in a controlled charge, their singleshot Springfield carbines spewing out a volley while riding at full speed. The bugler raised his instrument and the guidon carrier was by van Sillen's side, guidon in left hand, pistol in right.

"Boot carbines!" van Sillen roared. "Draw pistols!" He saw the hours of drill show their mark in the way his unblooded troop reacted and obeyed without fuss or flurry. "Bugler, the charge!"

No cavalryman could hear the notes of the charge without knowing the wild thrill of it. The men who rode with van Sillen might be young, barely more than recruits, but they were well trained and capable. Every man urged his horse on towards the Utes.

Then they were among the Indians and the wild mad melee of a mounted battle began. Red turned and bellowed a warning which held the fire of the Akins' crew. It would take better and steadier marksmen than any of the young dudes to call his shots on foe not friend in that wild and dust churning scene ahead.

Van Sillen's saber was in his right hand as he led his troop into the horde of Utes. He saw the painted face of a warrior before him and drove the point of the saber into it, then felt his horse charge into the Indian's mount and knock it from its feet. A lance thrust by him and the backhand slash of his saber almost tore the lance wielder's head from his shoulders.

The fight was general now, on foot and from horse-back. Red saw van Sillen's young second lieutenant, on foot, go down with a lance through his shoulders. The Ute who struck the blow dropped from his saddle and gripped the soldier by the head, knocked off his hat and was about to bring his scalping knife across. Red's Colts were empty and he holstered the right hand gun as he leapt forward. His boot lashed up, catching the Ute under the jaw, lifting him almost erect then throwing him over backwards. From the way the Ute's head snapped back Red thought he'd broken his neck but there was no time to worry. The shavetail's saber lay by his side and Red caught it up. He hefted the sword and gave the wild cavalry yell as he plunged into the thick of the fight again, showing that although not using a saber in a serious fight since the war, he'd kept up his practice with it.

Several of the Utes ran for the house, for the defenders were all mixed in the wild mill beyond it. The first to the open door started in and was blown out in the roaring blast of a shotgun. Van Sillen saw the Utes and sent his horse forward to leave its saddle and land on the porch, his saber slashing and driving the Indians before him. A brave leapt on to the porch behind him, a Dance Brothers revolver lining on the captain's back. Then he felt as if he'd been hit by a wildcat. Something crashed into his back, a hand digging into his lank black hair and another clawing at his face. Amanda Akins had seen van Sillen's danger and came to his aid with a fury of an enraged bobcat. Van Sillen heard the noise, sent his saber point into a Ute's chest, then turned and slashed at the brave Amanda still held. The girl let loose, staggering back to the wall, then bent and took up the old Dance Brothers gun, cocking it and holding it with both hands. Van Sillen bowed his head, ducking it down between the legs of the charging Ute and straightening to throw him over. He crashed on his back at Amanda's feet and the Dance gun bellowed in her hands. Old Dingle would have been pleased to know his revolver took the life of the man who killed him, for the .44 bullet smashed down into the head of the Ute.

At that moment, even as van Sillen thrust the scared girl back into the house, there sounded the wild notes of a bugle and under the command of the other lieutenant and Sergeant Flint almost all the remainder of the Fort's detachment came charging down into the attack.

Under this new threat the remaining Utes threw down their weapons, knowing their only chance lay in surrender. The Lazy D and Apache County was safe from Ute outrage, but the safety had been paid for in human lives. Four of Akins' hands were dead, three more wounded. Fifteen of the blue clad cavalrymen would never again answer muster call.

Red Blaze cleaned the blade of the saber on a dead Ute's breechcloth, some of the anger gone from him. He found Akins and van Sillen by his side.

"I sent a runner to the fort for reinforcements," the captain said.

"I'm surely pleased you did. There were more Utes than I expected. You've got a real good battalion there, Ran."

It was night and the moon was already rising before the wounded were tended and the business of cleaning up began. Sergeant Flint dragged a Ute to where his commanding officer stood with Akins and Red Blaze. At least the man appeared to be a Ute until his blue eyes, showing in the light of a lantern, told of his mixed blood.

"Found this breed among them." Flint growled. "Allow he knows something."

"You asked him?" inquired Red.

"I asked him. Gets all coy and allows he'll get word to that damned woman who was out here a couple of years back looking into the brutal way the Army treated the Injuns if we lay a hand on him. She'd like that, have a good excuse to come out and start again."

Red's hands shot out, gripping the front of the half-breed's shirt and hauling him forward. "Now listen good to me, breed. I'm not Army and politicians don't mean a thing to me. So you and me's going off under that tree out there a piece and we ain't going to waste time. You're either going to talk or I'm tossing a rope over a branch, fixing an end round your neck then hauling you up. After that you can either talk or hang until you rot."

The half-breed had been grinning, sure his threat would work. The grin died as he was hustled off away from the house. He was no weakling but in this moment was like a baby in Red's hands. Colonel Akins watched Red go and took a length of rope from where it lay, having been used to haul the bodies of the Utes away from the house. He followed Red, not with a morbid interest, or to be able to boast he helped hang an Indian, but as a man who was willing to back his neighbor in any play.

"Here'll do us, Colonel," Red said. "Toss the rope over the branch."

"You won't get away with it," snarled the half-breed, but his voice showed uncertainty and fear.

"Who'll know?" asked Red coldly. "Time anybody comes to look you'll be under a whole pile of dead Utes at the bottom of a hole. Don't reckon even that woman would want to look too careful at you then."

There was no defiance in the half-breed as he felt the rope slide around his neck and saw the two men grip the other end. "I'll talk!" he screamed.

Talk he did. He knew little enough except that his cousin, No-Nose, had got word to him to bring some bad hat warriors for a job. From what he'd heard he guessed that Hillvers wanted the Lipan reservation to make into a ranch and the Utes were to make the local citizens believe the Apaches could not be trusted. The attempts at killing Nogana and Johnny Raybold were supposed to start open hostilities, for Hillvers recognized the Texans as being chief stumbling block to his plans. It was No-Nose who made both tries, the half-breed claimed, and Red did not disbelieve him. Then the breed laid the finger on Hillvers for supplying the arms for this raid and told how Gren, Sharpe and No-Nose went after the girl who saw the arms delivered.

"You let me go now?" he asked.

Red's bunched fist shot out, smashing into the half-breed's face and sending him sprawling to the ground. Van Sillen and some of his men had been interested onlookers and the captain gave orders which sent his men forward to drag the half-breed to the storehouse in which the Utes were packed for the night under heavy guard.

"You wouldn't have gone through with it, would you, Red?" asked van Sillen.

Red Blaze's face was hard, the eyes no longer merry and the lips without their usual grin. "After what happened to Comanche Blake I'd kill every last one of them."

"We'll have to bring Hillvers in for trial," Akins remarked, bringing the business back to the most urgent matter of all.

"It won't be easy. He had five men at least at his back," warned van Sillen. "I'll use my men if you like."

"We don't like," Red put in. "This's a matter for Apache County to settle. In the morning I'm taking my boys into town and we'll get Hillvers, guns or no guns."

"Not without me along," barked Akins, "or without the authority of the county behind you. Gren forfeited his office by his actions today. I'm appointing you as sheriff, Red. If that's all right with you."

"It is. Tomorrow at dawn you and me'll go pick up the S-B crew and we'll see how things lay with Hillvers."

There was no point in Red's going to his home, even if he could collect his horse. Sue was not expecting him until the following morning and would be worried sick if she heard a rider approaching through the night.

The following morning, just after dawn, Red and Akins rode across the range towards the S-B ranch. The big rancher was grim as he nursed the shotgun across his knees. If there was shooting needed to take Hillvers. Akins meant to share in the risks of it.

Red knew there would be fighting. With a rope waiting for him Hillvers would not surrender. Red knew he could rely on Billy Jack who was fast with his guns and had tangled in corpse-and-cartridge affairs, but young Frank and Tex had never matched shots in the swirl of a gunfight. He did not wish to match them against Hillvers' hired guns. Akins had proved himself a man of some courage but he too had never gone up against the skill and training of hired killers, men who made their living with the smoking barrels of their weapons.

The S-B house came into view at last but there was something different about it. In one of the corrals were a dozen fine bloodhorses and grazing to one side a sight which gladdened Red's eyes. Two big stallions grazed free by the corrals, a paint and a black.

"That paint," Akins said, pointing ahead eagerly. "It's Captain Fog's horse, isn't it?"

"Nope, but somebody near on as good with his guns. We've got us a posse now."

Sue Blaze came racing from the Raybold house to throw her arms around Red's neck, her face showing signs of the sleepless night she'd spent. He kissed her, whispered everything was all right at the Lazy D, then gently moved her aside and went to meet the two men who came from the bunkhouse.

They were both tall, one a handsome blond boy in his teens. A boy with a spread to his shoulders and a tapering down at the waist. A boy in the dress of a tophand Texas cowboy and with a buscadero gunbelt with matched staghorn handled Colt Artillery Peacemakers in the holsters. The other was not quite so tall, slim, pallid of face, studious looking almost. Yet it was a tan resisting pallor, for he too wore the dress of a tophand, his coat's right side was stitched back to leave clear the ivory butt of the Civilian Model Peacemaker in the fast man's holster at his right side. That gun, like the matched brace of his companion, hung just right, spelling to the eyes which knew the signs, that here was a man who was real fast with his gun.

"Howdy Waco, Doc," Red greeted, his welcome less boisterous than it would have been in other circumstances.

"Betty told us," Waco replied, gripping Red's hand. "Allowed we'd be more use here than trying to help you or Lon. Lord. I'd like to lay my hands on the lousy bunch who shot that gal."

Waco's anger was cold and bitter. He was the youngest of Ole Devil's floating outfit and had been an orphan almost from birth. He'd ridden for Clay Allison as a hand and a man, or a boy, for that was all Waco had been, did not ride for the Washita curly wolf without being good with a gun. Waco was all of that and well along the path to becoming another Wes Hardin when he tied

in with Dusty Fog. Now to Dusty he gave devotion and
hero-worship which would have gone to the father he
never knew. To the other members of the floating outfit
he gave the loyalty of a younger brother to his elders.
He felt the killing of the Kid's girl as if he'd known
Comanche Blake all his life.

Doc Leroy was silent and grim. He was older than
Waco, a rider of the Wedge trail crew before joining the
O.D. Connected. Doc gained his name by two years of
study, reading medicine in an Eastern college. Then circumstances sent him home to Texas and riding the cattle
trails. His knowledge of doctoring work had been useful
and he was something of an expert at removing bullets,
as expert as he was at putting bullets in via his low tied
Colt.

"I want you to ride into town with me," Red told the
two men.

"I'll get the horses."

It was Waco's only comment. Why Red wanted them
to ride did not matter. That they were riding into trouble
was more likely, for Waco knew the signs. Red was on
the prod, not just a wild fling of temper at some chance
insult, but the cold and deadly prod of a lawman going
after a dangerous killer.

"It's to do with the Kid's girl?" Doc asked.

"Sure," replied Red.

"He doesn't deserve to live," was Doc's sole comment.

Hillvers was a worried man as he sat in his office and
looked at the Ute girl who had just come into town. The
clock on the wall showed ten past noon and the five
gunmen who lounged around the room were well aware
of the time. They looked hard, cold and dangerous; their
leader, his head still bandaged from where Dusty Fog's

pistol barrel laid him low, acted as interpreter.

"She says the Utes never got back from their raid," he said. "Took with all the soldiers being out of the fort, Gren, Sharpe and No-Nose being missing and what the squaw said about the Blake gal watching them it shapes up to a helluva lot of trouble, Hillvers."

"What're you fixing in to do about it?" went on another gunman, looking at Hillvers and forgoing, as had the interpreter, the usual "boss" when they spoke to the man who hired them.

"Clear out of here—and fast."

With that Hillvers came to his feet but the big gunman moved forward and blocked his path.

"You're forgetting something."

"What?"

"Money. Pay for us hard-working boys. You promised us a fair cut at the big jackpot and we want it, even if the jackpot didn't come."

Hillvers scowled, but his scowl died an uneasy death, for he knew the sort of men he was dealing with. Coates, the big gunman, and his friends had no scruples or they would never have backed his play against the white people when he used Utes. They would not hesitate to kill him if he crossed them.

"I haven't any money here. What's left after expenses is all at the bank."

"Which same's soon solved," Coates replied. "We'll go down and make a withdrawal right now."

"Sure, we'll do that."

It was the only answer Hillvers could make. At the bank was a small deposit, money which should have been used to purchase supplies and comforts for the Apaches' reservation.

"I'll go and collect the money."

"And we'll come with you."

That was not what Hillvers wanted. At the livery barn his horse was waiting for him and had been ever since he saw the second detachment of troops leave the fort. He'd been aware of a premonition of trouble and so took some money from its safe hiding place to lock in his desk ready for a hurried departure. If he could get away from his men he might be able to make a run for it and then return later to it. Now there was no chance of that. His Webley was in the shoulder clip but he knew he would have no chance against any one of the five men.

"Come on then," he growled. "Let's go."

The streets of the town were deserted as Hillvers walked along them with his five men. He cast a glance hopefully towards the jail. If Gren was there some difference in the plans for the gunmen might be made. This hope was dashed, for the jail was silent and empty. So Hillvers walked on towards the saloon, but before they reached it Coates caught his arm.

"Not frontways, Hillvers. We'll use the ladies' entrance for once."

The teller of the bank lifted the peephole cover and looked out, seeing only Hillvers, for the other men had moved to the sides and out of view. Hillvers was a good client and so the teller opened the door. He looked somewhat surprised when five men followed Hillvers in.

"I want to make a withdrawal, Charlie," Hillvers said.

"Certainly, Mr. Hillvers."

The teller was a newcomer to Apache County, one of Akins' party and yet he handled most of the work to do with the bank. He turned and opened the safe, not looking back at the gunmen and seeing nothing unusual in Hillvers bringing them with him. Opening the safe he started to turn.

"That's what we wanted."

Coates moved forward, his gun in his hand. The young teller started to rise, his mouth opening, but Coates moved forward, his Colt lifting and slammed down on to the young man's head. The teller slid down to the floor and lay still. Coates growled an order to his men to empty the safe and tie up then gag the teller.

Five minutes after entering the bank Coates and Hillvers came out, followed by the other men, making for the street once more and leaving an empty safe behind them. Hillvers was thinking furiously and cursing himself for getting into this. Nobody would believe he did not know the bank was to be robbed, that he was not the brains behind it.

They turned on to the street and came to a halt. Five men blocked their way, standing across the street. Red Blaze was in the center, his Spencer carbine in his hands. By his side at the right, looking grimly determined, was Colonel Akins holding a shotgun, and Billy Jack, hands hooked into his belt. To Red's left stood two strangers, two tall Texas cowhands whose stance and bearing told men who knew that they were supremely skilled with their guns.

Hillvers saw his chance, saw it and took it fast.

"Hold-up!" he roared, thrusting Coates to one side and leaping forward to race along the street. "They held up the bank!"

Staggering though he was, Coates drew his Colt and fired. His aim was off and the killing bullet struck Hillvers high in the right shoulder, making him stumble but not stopping him. Clutching his shoulder, Hillvers went between two buildings, knowing the wound was nothing more dangerous than a bad graze or he would not be on his feet. Behind him all hell tore loose on Geronimo

Street as the gunmen went for their guns.

Doc Leroy was first into action. His ivory handled Colt almost appeared to meet the white flutter of his boneless looking hand in midair. Flame lashed from the barrel and Coates went down as he tried to correct his aim and fight his way clear.

An instant behind Doc and ahead of Billy Jack, Waco's matched Colts were throwing lead into the first of the gunmen to start his draw after Coates. Billy Jack saw the man he picked to stop in middraw as the .45 bullet struck him between the eyes and slung him to the ground. The fourth man was caught by a .52 bullet from Red's carbine and the charge from Akins' shotgun and he was a tolerably dead man before he hit the ground. The fifth man completed his draw but threw his gun to one side and got his hands high, yelling he quit.

The smoke drifted from the scene. One gunman had surrendered, one badly wounded and three dead, mute testimony to the gunspeed and deadly accuracy of the Texas men. "Watch 'em, Colonel," Red snapped, levering a bullet into his Spencer and jacking back the big side hammer. "Don't take chances. Hillver's my meat."

Akins had been watching the way Red handled things and knew he would make a damned good county sheriff. Red had the training and ability to handle the post. True he was partner in a ranch but the extra money might come in useful, more so with the start of his family.

The men closed in with guns ready. Doc Leroy kicked the Colt away from Coates and looked down at the man. He was badly hit and would likely not live so Coates was determined Hillvers would not get away with anything. His last few moments were used in a snarled out confession of Hillvers' plans.

"The lily-livered rat," Coates snarled with his last breath. "Go get—"

He was dead before he could finish.

Red Blaze headed straight for the Indian Agency, for there he would find Hillvers, that he was sure of. Hillvers had made money on his running of the Agency and would not leave it behind him.

The guess was correct.

Hillvers reached the Agency as gun thunder shattered the peace of Apache City. He expected his men to make a long fight for it, but to make sure got the revolver out with his left hand. His right was limp and numb, useless to him unless he could get the wound treated.

Laying the gun on the desk he opened the cupboard and lifted out the carpetbag. There was no sound of shooting on the street now and he knew whichever way it went somebody would be looking for him. Even as the thought struck Hillvers he saw a shadow fall across the door and looked up, a snarl of fury on his face.

Red stood at the door, his Spencer in his hands, barrel pointing to the floor. There was a look on Red's face which sent Hillvers' hand crawling across the table to his revolver.

"I wasn't in the hold-up!" he croaked.

"I don't care," replied Red. "There's a wagon coming to town with Comanche Blake's body on it. Gren, Sharpe and that half-breed No-Nose killed her."

Hillvers heard the words even as his hands reached the butt of the Webley Bulldog revolver. He knew he would hang at least for what had happened to the girl. He gripped the gun and started to bring it up.

Red Blaze had seen the revolver, he waited until Hillvers had it and was swinging it around to line and shoot. Then Red brought the Spencer up hip high, his finger closed on the trigger, the side-hammer fell and the bullet tore through Hillvers' head.

CHAPTER THIRTEEN

The Hunting of Three Men

The Ysabel Kid rode to where Dusty Fog sat his big paint stallion and watched the opening, ready to prevent Gren's bunch leaving. The two friends looked at each other but said no word about their feeling of grief at the death of Comanche Blake. For all that the Kid knew he had Dusty's sympathy, knew Dusty and Mark would stay with him on this trail until the men who killed Comanche were dead.

"Where are they?" asked the Kid.

"On the reservation somewhere," Dusty answered. "You'll find their sign out there. Mark's gone ahead to ask Hunting Wolf to close the gaps and hold them in here for you."

"Let's ride."

The Kid said no more and started his horse through

the gap with Dusty following on his heels. The Kid held Comanche's carbine in his hands, he'd checked the gun was loaded and in working condition, now he held it ready. Once through the walls he halted for a moment. The tracks left by the three men were plain to see. Dusty could have followed them with ease, but he let the Kid handle it. Something, even the following of the tracks, must be done to prevent the Kid brooding and sinking out of his depth in grief. Revenge was the one thing keeping the Kid going and he must have something to do until time healed the raw wound.

Ahead of them, on the reservation, Gren and his two men rode with many a terrified backwards glance and the cold hand of death laying heavily on them.

"Is there any other way out of this basin?" gasped Sharpe.

"Sure, a few ways," replied No-Nose. "But you couldn't ride a hoss over many of them. I know one place we could ride through, or lead the hosses if we can't ride."

"Get us to it," snarled Gren.

The half-breed turned his horse and the other two followed him. They paid no attention in their panic in-spired flight, to the fast moving dust clouds which sped across the range in various directions, or the lights which flashed and the smoke that puffed up in a manner that no normal fire ever made. One of the dust clouds sped by them at a distance heading in the same direction they were going but none of them saw it, so intent were they on their flight.

Ahead the walls of the reservation rose steep and sheer but there was a place where they might ride out, a crack in the cliff which offered a steep path to the top. They might not be able to ride over it, but they could climb out on foot and lead their horses.

They were riding towards the crack when No-Nose brought his horse to a halt and pointed. Some dozen or more Apaches were among the rocks at the foot of the crack. Apaches who held rifles or bows and appeared to be determined to halt the three men. Gren looked nervously at the other two, then thought of the times he'd given orders to these same braves. He started his horse forward, intending to demand they were let through. One of the braves brought up his rifle and fired, the bullet screaming up in a ricochet before the three horses and bringing them to a halt. The Apaches were holding weapons ready and Gren knew he would not order his way by them.

"They know, Gren," No-Nose screamed. "They know what's happened. Let's get away from here and try another place."

The three horses turned and headed along parallel to the sheer walls while three scared sets of eyes scanned the rock for some way they might climb over. They did not see the lights which glinted, reflected by the sun and mirror, on the path, first in the center, then further across in the direction they were riding.

From far across the reservation Dusty Fog saw the light and caught the Kid's arm, bringing his gaze to the signal. The Kid read the meaning and without a word turned his horse at an angle which would bring him out either before, behind or right on top of Gren, Sharpe and No-Nose. Which it was mattered little to the Kid, for he was hunting the killers of his woman and time meant nothing to him.

Before they'd ridden a mile Dusty and the Kid saw two men riding towards them, each heading six horses. They were Mark Counter and Shinqua, bringing relay

mounts for the long hunt ahead. Not for the first time
the Kid was grateful for having such loyal friends.

"Rest your hoss, Lon," Mark said, "take one of the
relays."

The horses were the pick of the Apache remuda and
all owned by Shinqua. He was a man of some wealth by
Apache standards and, strangely for an Apache, selective
in the horses he owned. Not for Shinqua the multitude
of inbred, runty bangtails his fellows took. He would
rather own fewer horses and all of them good, big and
well bred stock. These horses were his pride and joy. It
said much for his respect that he allowed the three Texans
to use them.

With a fresh mount between his knees and the big
white stallion following, held in reserve for the final run
after the killers, the Kid rode on. Shinqua made no attempt to tell the Kid anything, seeing he had correctly
read the message of the flashing lights.

From fuirther along the wall, in the distance, they
heard the flat crack of rifles, then a puff of smoke rose,
telling that the men they hunted had tried another escape
route and found it blocked.

Once more Shinqua did not insult his Comanche brother
by indicating a direction for them to ride. If *Cabrito*
could not read the signs and make his own deductions
from them he was not worthy of being a member of the
Dog Soldier Lodge.

The four men rode on in silence. After a time they
reached the top of a slope and below saw three men
riding tired horses. They were Gren, Sharpe and No-
Nose, although their haggard faces were much different
in expression than when the other man last saw them.

The Kid gave a low whistle and his big white stallion
moved to his side. He left the carbine hanging by a

pigging thong through its ring and looped around the saddlehorn. Instead he drew the magnificent "One of a Thousand" Winchester from the saddleboot. He brought the weapon to his shoulder and aimed along the sights. The range was less than two hundred yards and the Kid knew his skill. He lined the rifle with care, his finger not quite touching the feather-light set trigger. The Kid's face might have been carved from rock for all the expression it showed, but his eyes glowed their hate.

All too well the Kid knew his capabilities. One touch of the trigger and Gren would be pitching from the saddle in the boned looking way a head-shot man always fell. Before his body hit the floor Sharpe would be falling after him and a bullet on its way to finish No-Nose. The Kid knew he was capable of doing it.

"No," he breathed, changing his aim slightly. "Comanche wouldn't want it that way. They've got to know who did it."

With that the rifle spat and Sharpe's hat spun from his head. The three men jerked round and their scared eyes looked up the slope. Then with a yell which was more of a fear-filled scream of terror, Gren put his spurs to his horse and sent it racing away. The other two were only an instant behind, going in blind fear and without looking behind them. If they'd looked they'd have seen their pursuers were not racing after them but merely following at the same even walk.

The Kid was still setting the pace, knowing there was no rush. The three men were penned in the basin and in time their fear would bring them into his hands. No longer was the Kid a white man, even though his clothes were the same. He was pure Comanche and using the oldest Comanche trick, making the killers of Comanche Blake pay time and over for their deed.

Expecting at any minute to see one of the number go down with lead in him Gren, Sharpe and No-Nose urged their horses on, ignoring the sweat which poured from the sweating hides and the froth which bubbled from their mouths. Something had to give. It was No-Nose who felt his horse quiver, then crumple forward. He kicked his feet free and lit down running, yelling to the other two. They looked back at him but made no attempt to halt. The same thought was in both their minds, throw No-Nose to the Ysabel Kid, allow him to cause a delay while they tried to find a way out of the box they were in.

No-Nose grabbed out his revolver and fired three shots after the others, then he turned and looked back. Terror welled up inside him, for he saw the Kid was riding forward faster. His eyes went to his horse, seeing it was down and lying on his booted Sharps rifle. He turned and started to run, making for where a scar in the land showed a dried up watercourse. The banks were some ten feet high, sloping down to a thickly bush covered bottom. No-Nose plunged down and hurled himself into the bushes as he heard the thunder of hooves above. He gripped his Colt and turned around, flattening out of sight, its butt held tight in his hand.

The Kid did not ride blindly into view on top of the rim. He came down from his horse and ran forward to go over the edge in a rolling dive. Twice as he went down the slope he heard shots and the slap of lead. At the bottom he was on his feet, knife in hand as he went into the bushes with a silent rush.

Now No-Nose was in a panic. He'd fired and missed, seeing the Kid go from view holding that razor edged knife. All too well No-Nose recalled what he'd heard of the Kid's skill in thick bush, how he could move in complete silence when hunting his prey. Somewhere in the bush that black dressed heller was moving, coming towards him. No-Nose was rigid with fear, not daring to move or make a sound for fear it would bring the Kid to him. In his hand the revolver weighed heavily and he cocked it, then whirled at some slight, possibly imagined, sound. A dull click was all that came from the Colt, for No-Nose had emptied it first after Gren and Sharpe, then at the Kid as he slid down the slope.

He flung the gun to one side and whipped out the saw-edged bowie knife. From the corner of his eye he saw a movement and whirled to find the Kid was almost on him, coming in with knife held ready. No-Nose let out a shriek of terror, then the Kid was on him.

On top of the watercourse, Dusty, Mark and Shinqua sat their horses and looked down at the bushes. They could see nothing and hear less for a few moments. Then they heard the rush of feet, a shriek, then a thrashing such as two cougars might make as they fought over a mate. At last a scream sounded, another. It was many long minutes until the screaming finally stopped.

The Ysabel Kid came from the bushes. His face expressionless under the dirt it gained in the roll down the slope. His shirt and trousers were also dirty and the shirt's sleeve torn. In his right hand he held the red-bladed bowie knife and in the left a gunbelt which supported a long barreled Colt in a half-breed holster and a saw-edged bowie knife. He plunged his knife blade into the sandy soil to clean it, then thrust it away. Then he walked up the slope and halted to look away across the reservation.

"That's the first," he said, but he was not speaking to the three silent men who watched him.

Mounting, the Kid looked around, but there was no

sign of lights to tell him in which way his enemies were traveling. Soon it would be dark and there would be no finding Gren and Sharpe before morning. They rode along the tracks left by the fleeing pair and shortly before dark an Apache scout stepped from where he'd been concealed in the bushes. He told how the two men had passed earlier, riding their all but played-out horses. There were two scouts and one went after the men, following them with orders to return when he found where they camped for the night as camp they must if they did not want to kill their horses.

"We'd best light down and rest," Mark suggested. "There's no way of following them in the dark."

The Kid nodded, swinging from his horse. The Apache scout made a small fire and produced jerked beef for them to eat. This and water was all they had so all made do with it. The Kid sat away from the others, cleaning his guns and looking into the fire. There would be no sleep for him that night. His grief would not let him rest until two more men were dead.

Gren and Sharpe rode through the darkness on their foot-weary horses. Behind them, unseen and unsuspected, the Apache brave had little trouble in following, even though on foot.

"We got to rest the hosses, Gren," Sharpe finally said.

"Happen we find them there's other ways out of the reservation," Gren answered tiredly.

Then the men knew they would have no trouble in finding the ways from the reservation. All around the walls fires were lit, clearly showing the ways out of the basin. The fires also showed even more clearly that no way out was left, for around them were Apache braves, alert and unsleeping. There was no way out, no way two exhausted men might sneak by those watching braves.

"We'll stop here," Gren growled as he allowed his horse to sink its head into the waters of a small stream.

Gren knew that the horses would go down as surely as had No-Nose's mount if they weren't given chance to rest. He shuddered at the thought of what fate held for the half-breed, now almost certainly dead. The same fate might be his own in a short time unless he was very lucky.

"We can make camp here for the night and move in the morning," he went on.

For all the words Gren did not mean to be here in the morning. After Sharpe was asleep he meant to take the two horses and move on, then hide until daylight and make a run for the main entrance to the reservation where he might take the guards by surprise. Sharpe, on foot, would fall easy prey to the Kid and would delay the pursuit.

So it was that two frightened men made their cold, foodless and fireless camp on the banks of the small stream and settled down to sleep. Sheer exhaustion caused Sharpe's eyes to close although he fought off the sleep as long as he could in a desperate attempt to stay awake until after Gren was safely sleeping. Sharpe's thoughts had been the same as Gren's but he fell asleep first and so failed to carry them out. Gren lay for a long time watching Sharpe, until sure he was sleeping and not likely to waken. Then the big man rose and went to the horses which stood saddled. Taking the reins in his hands he walked away, leading the horses with him. For four miles he walked until at last he dragged his exhausted body into a thick clump of bushes, tied the horses to a branch and slumped to the ground.

Sharpe's eyes opened as the light of dawn gave way to full daylight. He was stiff and sore, for a moment unsure of where he was or what he was doing. Then the recollection came back to him and he looked around. He was alone. Gren and the two horses were gone. He was left afoot!

"Gren!" he screamed.

"He's gone."

The words brought Sharpe spinning around, fear throwing speed into his scared movements. The black dressed shape at the edge of the bushes was real enough and must have been standing watching him for some time. Sharpe licked his lips as his eyes went to the carbine in the Ysabel Kid's right hand, barrel pointing to the ground.

The young Apache had done his work well. He'd waited until sure the white men were settling down and then returned by the most direct route to where his fellow scout waited for him. Then he returned with the others, showing them where Sharpe lay alone. Dusty, Mark and the Kid had not been surprised or unduly worried by seeing Gren had taken his departure, they could have guessed he would do so.

So the Kid and the others made camp not half a mile away and with the dawn he moved in to settle his account with the second of Comanche Blake's killers.

"Your pard run out on you," the Kid said. "Start your move when you're ready."

"I didn't kill the girl! It was Gren!"

"You were all on hand."

The words came in a flat, expressionless voice which warned Sharpe he could expect no mercy. He saw the other men standing behind the Kid, reading their flat hate in their eyes, knowing they were with the Kid in whatever he did.

"It was Gren! He shot her!"

"Count to three, Dusty," said the Kid as if Sharpe had never spoken.

"One!" said Dusty Fog.

Sharpe's hands lashed towards the butts of his guns, fear lending speed to his move. His hands were closing on the gun butts when the Ysabel Kid made his move. The Winchester carbine tilted up to slap the foregrip into the waiting left hand, then spewed flame while only hip high. Sharpe gave a startled and agonized grunt as the flatnosed bullet caught him in the chest, staggering him back. The Kid fired again and again, levering the bullets into the breech and firing them, slamming the reeling, staggering man before him. Nor did he stop until the carbine was empty. The doll rags which had been Sharpe hung on the bush into which he fell. It was a horrible sight, but the Kid walked towards it after tossing the carbine to Shinqua. Stripping off the bloody gunbelt, the Kid walked from the corpse. He buckled the belt and hung it with the other which was over his saddlehorn.

"That's two, Fire Bird," he said.

"Gren took both the horses, went this way," Dusty remarked.

"He couldn't get out, could he, Shinqua?" Mark asked in Spanish.

"No man can get out of here without I give the word," was the reply.

"Then we'll go look for him."

It was the Kid who spoke. He swung afork one of the Apache horses which had been fetched by the braves, whistled to his white and rode forward with his eyes on the ground.

The Kid took the trail again, reading the signs with the others following and looking for signal lights or some sign they might use to take them to Gren. The reservation was still, no keen-eyed scout could see Gren. It was as if the earth had opened and swallowed him.

"Still on foot," Mark said. "His hosses are near on done."

"More likely laid up ahead there," guessed Dusty.

Shinqua moved forward to the Kid's side and for the first time spoke directly to him. "Revenge is good, Comanche brother. But when it is done a man would be better if he forgot it and what caused it."

"You speak the words of wisdom, Shinqua," replied the Kid, also speaking Apache. "When this is over I will ride away and never come to this place again."

"If your friends have need of your help you will come. She-who-is-gone would not have it any other way."

The Kid did not reply even though he knew Shinqua was speaking the truth. If the S-B ever needed help and Ole Devil's floating outfit rode, the Kid would ride with them. Comanche would want her man to stand by his friends.

Suddenly the Kid brought his horse to a halt. The big white stallion by his side had stopped, thrown back its head and snorted. It was an old and well learned trick, this warning of hidden men and one the Kid never regretted his horse knowing. Ahead was a thick clump of bushes in which a man and two horses might easily be hidden. The Kid was alert and so were the other men.

There was a scared yell, a crashing, and a rider burst from the bushes. It was Gren and he was racing his horse away as fast as spur could make it go, forgetting his weapons, leaving them in leather as he raced away to try and save his worthless life.

The Kid gave a whistle and the white stood like a statue. Then he left the Apache horse and landed on his double girthed Texas saddle and the white came from a halt to a dead gallop within three strides. The rest followed, not hurrying, for it was the Kid's duty to take Gren alone. All wondered by what method the big burly killer was to die.

Gren heard the thunder of hooves behind him and tried to urge more speed from his horse. He might just as well have been on foot for all the good his horse did him now. The huge white stallion closed the distance between itself and the horse Gren rode as if the other was standing still. Even fresh Gren's horse would have stood no chance against that white stallion the Kid called Blackie. Right now the other horse, tired from the neglect of the previous day, was slowing. Gren was wild with panic, screaming curses, and kicking his spurred heels into the flanks of the horse and drawing his Smith and Wesson to make a fight for his life.

The Kid came nearer with every raking stride of his horse. He left his rifle in the saddleboot and his old Colt Dragoon holstered at his side. This was the man who sent at least one shot into Comanche Blake and he did not deserve the honorable death a bullet would give.

Reaching down the Kid unstrapped his rope, the sixty foot length of hard plaited Manila which was always at his saddlehorn. He shook loose the loop, made sure the leather wrapped eyelet was free and the rope would run through it easily. Then he measured the distance with his eye and lashed the necessary length of rope securely to his saddlehorn in the way of a Texas man who aimed to hang on to whatever he caught. He measured the distance between himself and the fleeing Gren and was satisfied. The Kid gave the loop a quick twirl before him, round to the right, then up and over his head. His aim was made and he sent the loop sailing out, using his wrist to turn it and make it fly flat with the honda sliding and tightening the space as it sped towards its target. This was the hooley-ann throw used by the cowhand to snake his horse out of the remuda bunch in a corral. It was a throw to be made with neither fuss nor excitement to the other horses. It was strictly a head catch and for Gren's bare head the loop was flying.

The Kid's aim was good, the rope's loop dropped over Gren's neck. Then the Kid brought his horse in a swinging halt, churning up the ground as it stopped. Gren's horse raced on, even as his hands went up towards the rope. He was too late. The rope snapped tight, held rigid by the great white stallion and the strength of the double girthed Texas saddle. It snapped down, the loop closing with all the finality of a hangman's noose around Gren's fat throat. He hit the end of the rope, a rope strong enough to take the full power of a longhorn bull's charge without any sign of snapping.

Gren was jerked backwards. His feet left the stirrups a fraction too late. There was an audible crack as the neck broke, then Gren's body was free of the saddle and for a moment it seemed to hover in the air, then it crashed down. The angle the neck hung at was a sure sign that Gren would never rise again.

The Kid swung down from his saddle and walked forward with his eyes cold and expressionless. He whistled and the white slacked the rope, allowing him to loosen the loop where it bit into Gren's throat. Then the Kid removed the gunbelt with the Smith and Wesson revolver and walked to his white without a second glance at the man he had killed.

Strapping the gunbelt with the other two on his saddle, the Kid vaulted astride the big white, hooked his foot over the saddlehorn and coiled his rope.

"That's the last. Rest easy, Fire Bird," he said.

It was sundown in Apache City and the streets were deserted, for every man, woman and child in the county who could make it now stood with heads bowed in the graveyard. They'd come in response to the riders Colonel Akins sent around with the word and they came to pay their last respects to a girl who a few days before they would have called a slut if nothing worse. All knew the debt they owed this wild girl called Comanche Blake. All knew the Akins family were alive this evening only through the girl's bravery and self sacrifice.

The pall bearers who carried the coffin had been Colonel Akins, Red Blaze, who now wore the badge of county sheriff. Captain van Sillen in full uniform, Johnny Raybold, defying the doctor's orders, Hacker Bland who forgot his illness for this duty, and a tall, blond Texas boy whose only name was Waco. They carried the coffin and lowered it into the grave. The burial service was read and the grave was about to be filled when three men came into the graveyard.

The mourners fell back to allow the three men through. The people in their sober black stood back as Dusty Fog, Mark Counter and the Ysabel Kid walked from the gate to the grave. There was no sound, for all knew how things had been between Comanche Blake and that hard faced, black dressed young Texan who walked between his friends and carried three gunbelts over his arm.

Every eye was on the three men as they came to a halt at the head of the grave. The silence could almost be felt as the men remembered Akins telling them the Ysabel Kid was hunting the men who killed Comanche, but no man dare ask or even say a word.

The Kid stood for a long five minutes, silent, stiff and paying his last respects to Comanche. His hat was thrust back to hang on its stormstrap and his face was set in a hard expressionless mask, only his eyes showing the grief he felt. He'd been taken by Dusty and Mark to the S-B house to collect their belongings, to wash and shave, then change into fresh clothes before riding to town. After this visit to the graveyard they would ride on, heading away from an area which held so much bitter memory for the Kid.

Slowly the Kid moved, taking the first gunbelt and throwing it into the open grave on to the coffin. It was a belt the crowd recognized, with a Colt in a half-breed holster and a saw-edged bowie knife. The second belt dropped after it, a belt with matched guns in the holsters. Then the third belt fell, a belt with a fancy Smith and Wesson Russian revolver in its holster. The three gunbelts fell on to the pine lid of the coffin, each thudding home, sounding louder than a cannon as they landed. Not one person in that crowd needed to know or ask to whom the gunbelts belonged.

Dusty made a sign to Waco and Doc Leroy and they moved towards him. Betty was with him, listening to his whispered good-bye as behind them the parson gave the sign for the filling of the grave to begin. The Kid turned on his heel and, followed by his four friends, made for the horses ready to ride back home to Texas. They swung into their saddles, turned and rode away into the coming night.

In the graveyard the dirt was covering the lid of the coffin and the three gunbelts. The men who killed her were dead and proof lay on her coffin. Comanche Blake's girl could rest easy in her grave.

J.D. HARDIN

"THE MOST EXCITING WESTERN WRITER SINCE LOUIS L'AMOUR" —JAKE LOGAN

___	872-16840-9	BLOOD, SWEAT AND GOLD	$1.95
___	872-16842-5	BLOODY SANDS	$1.95
___	867-21039-7	SONS AND SINNERS	$1.95
___	872-16869-7	THE SPIRIT AND THE FLESH	$1.95
___	867-21226-8	BOBBIES, BAUBLES AND BLOOD	$2.25
___	06572-3	DEATH LODE	$2.25
___	06138-8	HELLFIRE HIDEAWAY	$2.25
___	06380-1	THE FIREBRANDS	$2.25
___	06410-7	DOWNRIVER TO HELL	$2.25
___	06001-2	BIBLES, BULLETS AND BRIDES	$2.25
___	06331-3	BLOODY TIME IN BLACKTOWER	$2.25
___	06248-1	HANGMAN'S NOOSE	$2.25
___	06337-2	THE MAN WITH NO FACE	$2.25
___	06151-5	SASKATCHEWAN RISING	$2.25
___	06412-3	BOUNTY HUNTER	$2.50
___	06743-2	QUEENS OVER DEUCES	$2.50
___	07017-4	LEAD-LINED COFFINS	$2.50
___	06845-5	SATAN'S BARGAIN	$2.50
___	06850-1	THE WYOMING SPECIAL	$2.50
___	07259-2	THE PECOS DOLLARS	$2.50
___	07257-6	SAN JUAN SHOOTOUT	$2.50
___	07379-3	OUTLAW TRAIL	$2.50
___	07392-0	THE OZARK OUTLAWS	$2.50
___	07461-7	TOMBSTONE IN DEADWOOD	$2.50
___	07381-5	HOMESTEADER'S REVENGE	$2.50

Prices may be slightly higher in Canada.

 BERKLEY *Available at your local bookstore or return this form to:*
Book Mailing Service
P.O. Box 690, Rockville Centre, NY 11571

Please send me the titles checked above. I enclose _____ . Include 75¢ for postage and handling if one book is ordered; 25¢ per book for two or more not to exceed $1.75. California, Illinois, New York and Tennessee residents please add sales tax.

NAME _____

ADDRESS _____

CITY _____ STATE/ZIP _____

(allow six weeks for delivery.)